GHOSTS IN THE MIRROR

Alain Robbe-Grillet

GHOSTS
IN THE MIRROR

Translated by Jo Levy

JOHN CALDER · LONDON

First published in Great Britain in 1988 by
John Calder (Publishers) Limited
18 Brewer Street, London W1R 4AS

Originally published in France under the title
Le miroir qui revient by Les Editions de Minuit, Paris, 1984.

Copyright © Les Editions de Minuit 1984
Copyright © English translation Jo Levy 1988

British Library Cataloguing in Publication Data
Robbe-Grillet, Alain
   Ghosts in the mirror.
   1. Robbe-Grillet, Alain—Biography
   2. Novelists, French—20th century—
Biography
   I. Title   II. Le miroir qui revient
   English
   843'.914   PQ2635.0117Z

ISBN 0-7145-4093-5
ISBN 0-7145-4094-3 Pbk

Typeset in 11 on 12 Baskerville by Grassroots, London N3
Printed in Great Britain by Billing & Sons Ltd, Worcester

TABLE OF CONTENTS

11

If I remember rightly, I began writing this book a few months after the publication of *Topologie d'une cité fantôme*, towards the end of 1976 or the beginning of 1977. And now here we are in the Autumn of 1983 and the work has hardly progressed; the forty odd manuscript pages have always been abandoned for tasks that seemed more urgent. Two novels have appeared in the meantime, and a film—*La belle captive*—finished in January this year, screened in mid February. So, nearly seven years have gone by since I began with the words: 'I've never spoken of anything but myself...'—provocative at the time. The lighting has changed, perspectives shifted, in some cases inverted; but in fact the same questions still come up, perennial, haunting, maybe pointless...Let's try again seriously, one more time, before it's too late.

Who was Henri de Corinthe? I've already said I don't think I ever met him, except possibly when I was a very small child. But sometimes, when I do have memories of those brief interviews (in the strict sense of the word: as if through a door accidentally left ajar) I feel my fertile memory could be playing tricks and I might have invented them after the event, if not totally at least from the scrappy accounts whispered in the family or floating around the old house.

M. de Corinthe, Comte Henri—as my father mostly called him with an intangible blend of irony and respect—often came to see us, I'm almost sure...Often? Today I really can't work out how often. For example did he come every month? Or more often? Or did he only visit once or twice a year, his appearances—although fleeting—making such a vivid, lasting impression that everyone thought they were more frequent. And when did these visits actually stop?

But above all, what could he be doing in our house? What secrets, plans, needs, what kind of expectations or fears would associate him with my parents when everything—including rank and fortune—seemed to separate them? Living such an adventurous life, how and why did he find time to stay for a few hours (a few days?) in such a modest home? Why did my father seem to await his unpredictable arrival with a sort of fervent hope? Whereas when I peeped through the gap in the heavy red living-room curtains I saw him with the illustrious visitor looking worried, grief stricken. And also, although they never admitted it, why did they so obviously try and stop me meeting him?

It's probably with this albeit uncertain end in view—an attempt at answering such questions as these—that I started writing this autobiography some time ago now. And as I begin reading over the opening pages after a fatal lapse of seven years, I can hardly tell what I wanted to talk about so urgently. This is what happens with writing: at once a lonely, dogged almost timeless pursuit and an absurd submission to the, as it were, 'worldly' preoccupations of the moment.

Now at the beginning of the Eighties, there's been a sudden, violent reaction against any attempt to escape the norms of traditional expression-representation; so, my imprudent remarks of not so long ago no longer act abrasively to counter a new dogma that was creeping in (anti-humanism), but merely seem today to be sliding down the slippery slope of the prevailing discourse which has been re-instated: the good old eternal discourse of the past that I had at the outset fought against so passionately. In the wave of 'regression' breaking over us my wish, on the contrary, to pass beyond, to 'relieve the old guard' is likely to pass unnoticed.

And so should we now resume the terrorist activities of the years 1955-60? Certainly we should. And yet, (I'll explain why later), I persist in copying out these opening lines just as I wrote them in 1977 without changing anything; they are already old fashioned in my opinion, since they have so quickly become fashionable.

I have never spoken of anything but myself. From within and so this has hardly been noticed. Fortunately. Since in the space of one line I've just used three suspect, shameful, deplorable terms which I myself have largely assisted in discrediting, and this is enough to condemn me once again in the eyes of several of my peers and most of my descendants: 'myself', 'within', 'spoken of'.

The second of these apparently innocuous little words alone

tiresomely resurrects the humanist myth of depth (*bête noire* for us authors), while the last stealthily brings up the myth of representation whose contentious case drags on forever. As for the ever detestable 'myself', here it is certainly paving the way for an even more frivolous comeback: biography.

So, it's no coincidence that at this precise moment I agree to write a 'Robbe-Grillet by Robbe-Grillet',[1] which a short while ago, I would definitely have preferred to leave to others. Everyone nowadays knows that the notion of an author belongs to reactionary discourse—dealing with the individual, private property, profit—and that the work of the writer is, on the contrary, anonymous: merely a matter of combinations which could, at a pinch, be left to a machine since they seem so easily programmable; the human intention being depersonalised in its turn so that it only appears now as a particular phase in the class struggle which is the mainspring of History in general, as well as the history of the novel.

I myself have done much to promote these reassuring idiocies, and have now decided to refute them because I feel they've had their day: within the space of a few years they have lost any shocking, corrosive and, therefore, revolutionary force and so have been assimilated as ready-made ideas, still fuelling the spineless militancy of fashionable magazines, yet with a place already prepared for them in the glorious family vaults of the literary text books. Ideology, always masked, changes its face with ease. It's a hydra-headed mirror: whenever one head is cut off it soon springs up again, presenting the adversary with his true face in the mirror, which he believed he had defeated.

Copying his strategy, I'm going to make use of the monster's

---

1. This volume was originally planned for the *Ecrivains de toujours* series, published by Seuil (hence the mention below of 'the publishers opposite'). I even had a contract with Paul Flamand, which is still valid. It is only the unexpected turn the text took as it was being composed that made it unsuitable for the series of little books with their prescribed dimensions and numerous illustrations and for which I am therefore doing something quite different, concurrently.

remains too: see through his eyes, hear through his ears and speak through his mouth (steep my arrows in his blood). I don't believe in Truth. It only serves bureaucracy that is, oppression. The moment a bold theory stated in the heat of battle has become dogma it instantly loses its attraction and violence and, by the same token, its efficacy. It ceases to ferment liberty, discovery; nicely and thoughtlessly, it contributes one more stone to the edifice of the established order.

And so it's time to pursue other tracks and turn the fine new theory inside out in order to rout out the incipient bureaucracy it's secretly harbouring. Now that the *nouveau roman* defines its values positively, decrees its laws, brings its recalcitrant pupils back to the fold, enlists its guerillas, excommunicates its free thinkers, there's a pressing need to call everything into question and put the pieces back as they were: we need to take writing back to its starting point, the author back to his first book: in the modern narrative we must once more question the ambiguous part played by the representation of the world and the expression of a *person* who is simultaneously a physical body, a conscious projection and an unconscious.

I've been asked so often in interviews and symposia why I write, I ended up seeing the question as belonging to the realm of sense, of *ratio* that attempts to impose its intellectual laws (and so its dictatorship) on an activity that is dynamic and therefore always elusive. And in order to fill the silence from which writing comes I simply threw out various idle banalities, devious suggestions that led nowhere, or substituted scintillating metaphors for aphorisms. This was better than scraps of a catechism anyway.

But now I've decided to take a sidelong look at myself in the space of a small book, the new perspective has suddenly freed me from my old defences and reticence. I feel so bound up with the life and adventures of the Editions de Minuit that speaking about myself from the publishers opposite, I feel a completely new kind of freedom; I'm lighthearted, cheerful as an irresponsible narrator.

Consequently no definitive, no merely truthful explanation

of my written work and films should be expected from these pages (a definitive explanation straight from the author's mouth!)— how they really work, their real significance. I've said I'm not a truthful soul but nor do I tell lies, which would come to the same thing. I'm a sort of resolute, ill-equipped, imprudent explorer who doesn't believe in the previous existence or stability of the country in which he is mapping out a possible road, day by day. I'm not an intellectual guru, but a companion on the path of discovery and hazardous research. And here I am still venturing on a work of fiction.

When I was a child, for a long time I thought I didn't like the sea. Every night I drifted off to look for a tranquil, unfenced garden to fall asleep in, and the image of the paternal Haut-Jura formed most often in my mind: a hollow filled with moss grown rocks, or lined with cushions of saxifrage, gentle slopes, foothills covered in short grass, smooth as a park sown with gentians and soldanellas, where large fawn-coloured cows moved about slowly to a peaceful tinkling of bells among patches of immutable forest, like a stage set. Order, Rest. Everlasting quiet. I could abandon myself to sleep.

The ocean was turmoil and uncertainty, a realm of insidious perils where flabby, viscous beasts mingled with the muffled sound of the waves. And this is precisely the ocean that filled the nightmares I fell into the moment I lost consciousness, soon to wake up with screams of terror which didn't always dispell these confused phantoms that I couldn't even describe. My mother gave me linctus of bromide. Her obvious anxiety in some way confirmed the dangers I had only escaped from for the time being, which were lying in wait for me again in the dark, lurking behind my own eyes. Hallucinations, nocturnal delirium, intermittent sleepwalking—I was a calm child who slept restlessly.

We lived for a part of the year in my maternal family's house where I was born; a big house surrounded by a walled garden that seemed huge at the time; it was on the outskirts of Brest in what was then the country. From the windows in the room where I slept, you could see the whole Rade de Brest above the

17

trees. On our walks which sometimes lasted several days, we went from Brignogan, the river mouth, Saint Mathieu and the Ile d'Ouessant right up to the Pointe du Raz—in the wind, along the cold beaches, across heaps of jumbled rocks or along the crumbling, slippery coastguard paths on the edge of the precipice.

We spent August in a little village on the Quiberon peninsular and there too we preferred the *Côte Sauvage;* it really was still wild before the war and we were only too ready to believe the legends: whirlpools with subterranean crevices leading to the open sea where you could drown, your legs tugged under by the long strands of seaweed coiling round them; flood tides trapping you at the foot of a smooth vertical wall; waves from the deep reaching right up to the top of the highest cliff, sucking you down and swallowing you up. Needless to say I didn't learn canoeing or sailing, I've never even learnt to swim. In the mountains with no ski slopes or ski lifts, when I was twelve, I was perfectly at ease and quite reckless on my skis.

Any amateur psychologist will be delighted to recognise in the facile contrast between the Jura and the Atlantic—gentle vale cushioned with mossy hollows *versus* bottomless pit where the octopus lies in wait—the two traditional, opposed images of the female sex. I wouldn't like him to think that he's discovered this unbeknown to me. And, while we're about it, let's draw his attention to the phonetic similarity of *vague—vagin* (wave—vagina) and also to the etymology of the word nightmare whose root *mare* means sea in Latin, but in Dutch: nocturnal phantoms.

The room where my bed was in the small Parisian flat in the Rue Gassendi was separated by a glass double door from the dining-room where my mother would stay up reading her massive daily dose of papers till late in the night; they ranged from *La Liberté* to *L'Action française* (my parents were extreme right wing anarchists). The translucent red curtain which left me in relative darkness, was held open by the back of a chair so that she could keep close watch over my broken sleep. Her gaze, which reached me from time to time above the outspread newspaper, would disturb my solitary pleasures which already had a strong sadistic tendency. As for the ghosts, they usually appeared opposite me, in a corner of the ceiling, on the same

18

side as the reddened glass-panes; they advanced in steady waves in the pale part of the wall, between a cornice of acanthus leaves and the picture rail bordering the green wallpaper. The recurrent hallucination moved from left to right in a series of spirals or little waves, or more accurately, like the ornamental frieze sculptors call Vitruvian scrolls. What terrified me was when their seemingly orderly ranks began to tremble, disintegrate and twist in all directions. But the first steady sinusoid was already enough to frighten me, I so dreaded what was coming next.

It strikes me that I've been saying all this for a long time now, both in my books and films and doing so in a more accurate and convincing way. Obviously this hasn't been noticed, or hardly at all. Obviously, it's never bothered me: that wasn't the point of writing.

And yet today, I feel some pleasure in using the traditional autobiographical form: the ease mentioned by Stendhal in his *Souvenirs d'égotisme,* compared with the resistance of the material that characterises all creativity. And I'm interested in this questionable pleasure in that it confirms on the one hand that I began writing novels to exorcise the ghosts that I couldn't come to terms with and, on the other hand, I now see that fiction has, after all, a much more *personal* bias than the so-called sincerity of confession.

When I re-read sentences like 'My mother kept close watch over my broken sleep', or 'Her gaze would disturb my solitary pleasures', I have an irresistible urge to laugh; as if I were falsifying my past life in order to make it into a nice conventional object according to the canons of the late lamented *Figaro littéraire:* logical, affecting, malleable. Not that these details are inaccurate (far from it). But what's wrong is that there aren't enough of them, and they read like a work of fiction; in a word, I don't like what I would call their arrogance. I didn't live them in the imperfect tense, nor with particular adjectives in mind, and what's more, when they appeared in reality they were swarming in the midst of an infinite number of other details, the interwoven threads forming a living web. Whereas now, I pick out

19

a paltry dozen, each set up on its pedestal, cast in the bronze of a quasi-historical narrative (the past historic is not far away) and arranged in a causal sequence precisely conforming to the ideological tyranny against which my whole work rebels.

We're beginning to see more clearly. First rough point: by describing accurately the nocturnal monsters that threaten to invade my waking life I am writing in order to destroy them. But—second point—all reality is indescribable, and I know instinctively that consciousness is structured like our language (and with good reason!)—not so for the world, nor the unconscious. I can't use words and phrases to describe what's in front of me, nor what's lurking in my head or my sex. (Let's leave cinematic images aside for the moment, I shall demonstrate later—if I think of it—that they pose the same problem, contrary to what people think).

Literature is then—third position— the pursuit of an impossible representation. Knowing this, what can I do? All I can do is organise stories which are neither metaphors of reality nor analogues but act as *working constructs*. Then the ideology which governs our common consciousness and language structures will no longer be a constraint, the source of failure, since I've reduced it to the status of material.

With this perspective I can see my plan to tell my life story in two different contradictory ways. Either I insist on grasping the truth, pretending to believe that language can do this (which is the same as admitting language is free) and, in that case, all I shall ever produce is a *ready-made life story*. Alternatively, I shall replace the biographical details with working constructs explicitly expressing an ideology, but over these and thanks to these I shall this time be able to exercise my influence. The second method produces *La jalousie* or *Projet pour une révolution*. The first, alas, the present work.

No, that's not quite true either, since it will by now be obvious that this work isn't going to be restricted to a few trite memories offered as gospel truth. On the contrary, it must accompany me from critical essay to novel, from book to film, continually questioning, and the sea and fear will also then be mere working constructs in the text; and not solely in such and such a work mentioned, where these textual objects determine theme or structure, but also in this treatise itself which is why I previously called it fiction.

I was talking about fear. Very early on it was to play a large part in my infrequent reading as an adolescent. My sister (who read a lot) and I (who always read the same books over and over again) had been brought up on English literature from an early age. I've often mentioned Lewis Caroll as one of the main companions of my youth. More rarely I've spoken of Rudyard Kipling whose *Kim* and *Jungle Book* were not as precious to me as his Indian tales and, more precisely, the ones where soldiers were terrorised by morbid apparitions. Without having laid eyes on them for thirty or forty years I could retell the story of the legion lost in the night meeting another British patrol that had been wiped out in an ambush long ago. I can still hear the clash of the hooves of the horses of a hundred dead horsemen stamping on the mountainside as they stumble over the stones that mark their own graves. Also the story of Colonel Gadsby parading at the head of his regiment, who constantly sees himself falling from the saddle, crushed under the feet of the thousand horses of his dragoons riding at full gallop behind him. And that other officer pursued by a phantom rickshaw in which an abandoned mistress is weeping, driven to suicide by despair. Or the man who in 42°C in the shade puts a sharp spur in his bed in an attempt to escape the frightful visions—never described—to which he falls prey the moment he goes to sleep and which finally kill him.

I grew up on intimate terms with these spectres. They were quite simply part of my normal world, mixed up with spirits from Breton legends or from the ghost stories my maternal grandmother's sister our 'godmother', used to tell us in the evening to send us to sleep: sailors lost at sea coming back to drag the living from their beds by the feet, the *ankou*'s cart whose creaking and jolting announces the imminent death of the man lost at night in a web of sunken lanes that he thought he knew; enchanted spaces, bewitched objects, omens and signs, not to

21

mention the countless lost souls keening on the heaths or in the marshes who rattle the shutters of your room till daybreak when there isn't a breath of air and stir up the water in the bowls where the washing's been left to soak.

As the years and the stories went by, this family continued to grow, ever ready to welcome new presences quite naturally: from Corinthe's pale fiancée to the cursed Dutchman on the deck of his unmanned ship rushing through the night, his red sails spread over the phosphorescent waves. And here comes the ocean back again already. O Death, old captain, it is time to weigh anchor...

And there's the young Comte de Corinthe battling with the rising tide, riding his white horse, its sparkling mane interlaced with the spray, storm-torn from the crest of the waves. And there's Tristan, wounded, delirious, waiting in vain for the ship that will bring back Iseult la Blonde to Léon. And now there's Caroline de Saxe, her lifeless body drifting among the golden, rippling seaweed.

Characters in novels or films are also kinds of phantoms: you can see or hear them, you can never grasp them, if you try you pass right through them. Their existence is suspect, insistent like that of the unquiet dead forced by some evil spell or divine vengeance to live the same scenes from their tragic destiny over and over again. So Mathias in the *Voyeur* for instance, whom I've often come across wheeling his cranky bike on the cliff paths among tufts of close-cropped gorse, would simply be a wandering soul, just like the absent husband in *La jalousie* and the heros who so obviously come from the land of shades who people *Marienbad, L'immortelle* or *L'homme qui ment*. Anyway, this is one of the most plausible ways of 'explaining' why they don't look 'natural', why they seem remote, disoriented, out of place; an explanation for their relentless pursuit of goodness knows what, a quest which they seem unable to abandon or carry through as if they were desperately trying to gain access to a fleshly existence which is denied them, trying to enter a veracious world which is closed to them, or else attempting to drag the *other*, all the others, including the innocent reader into their impossible quest. Stephan Dedalus, K the surveyor, Stavrogin or the Brothers Karamazov lived like this. Labyrinthine paths, marking time, scenes that are repeated over and over again (even death can no longer ever be final), changeless bodies, timelessness, multiple spatial dislocations, finally the theme of the 'double' which informs a whole section of our literature and structures *L'homme qui ment* as well as *L'Eden et après* or the *Triangle d'or*— aren't these precisely the distinctive signs and natural laws of the eternal regions of the possessed?

I didn't know Henri de Corinthe personally. I probably never even saw him, as I imagine now, in those early years of my childhood spent in the *Maison Noire* where, as my father told me, he came from time to time on a neighbourly visit in the evening before retiring for the night.

At that time I thought the old house where I was born got its name from the dark granite façade which was so smooth and hard that no moss or lichen had taken hold on its high, vertical wall, except in the joins between the carefully fitted rectangular blocks. When the winter drizzle dampened the surface they gleamed like coal in the grey branches of the beech trees where, here and there, tenacious russet leaves still clung in the everlasting drizzle.

Corinthe would come up the long straight drive between the two rows of vertical boles, like the pillars in underground reservoirs in Constantinople in the engraving which graced my room at the head of the bed. His horse's hooves made no sound on the sodden ground as he approached in a sort of silent dance as if space, saturated with water, had relieved him of his own weight.

My father said that whether on foot or riding his white horse, the man always appeared like this: no sound of heel, sole or horseshoe signaled his approach: it was as if his heavy boots and the horse's hooves were clad in a thick layer of felt; unless they both had the power to move about without touching the ground, a few millimeters above the road or the black stone steps of the staircase or the flagstone floor of the vast dark room at the back of which he is now standing in front of the monumental fireplace where big oak logs are burning; his tall silhouette is elongated by the firelight, lighting him from behind, while his huge shadow, flickering with the flames, lengthens, turns paler and paler, reaches to the foot of the stairs which my father, called by a servant, is now descending to go to his late visitor who is holding out his frozen limbs to the ever-changing colours in the hearth.

Guttering paraffin lamp, will-o'-the-wisp over the marshes, pale rider gliding through the mist, bubbling water, close by a great bird's quick cry of alarm piercing the night, the sudden crackling of the fire breaking out among the dying embers...Angélica ...Angélica ...Why did you leave me, little flame? Who will console me for your light laugh?

I'm alone in my room. I listen to the nocturnal sounds surrounding the too spacious empty house on all sides. My dark window's swaying in the wind, framing the bare tree tops crowning the beeches. But over the rustle of the branches against the uncurtained window-panes, louder than the rain trickling in the valleys and gutters, rising above the heartrending calls of owl or weasel, I can hear muffled thuds from the bowels of the building like the clash of waves thrusting against the raised hull of a boat that drops back into the trough, thuds that seem to come out of the floor, the granite walls, the ancient earth itself, repeated blows, persistent, regular, which must be the slow beating of my own heart.

Down below in the vast flagstoned room whose dim boundaries are defined by the darkness alone, my father paces up and down while the memory of the Comte de Corinthe gradually fades. Neither of them say a word, each is rapt in his own thoughts, each is alone ...The blurred image stays for a few moments more, harder and harder to make out ...Then, nothing.

The above passage must be a complete fiction. The family house was simple, relatively large, sheltered by a few trees, but built of wattle and daub since the navy didn't allow anything more substantial in this zone, which was then under the jurisdiction of the naval base. However, the repeated thuds shaking the ground are definitely part of my childhood impressions. They could be heard particularly at night, every night for months on end. The hypothesis most often proposed by our grandparents, who were also worried by this phenomenon which was never officially explained, was that this was the result of the excavation work being carried out under the cliffs by the naval engineers, like some giant mole, for the purpose of installing vast underground reservoirs to store the fuel oil needed by our battle fleet. There was a large fleet based in Brest at that time. The whole town and its surroundings seemed to be under the supreme, mysterious rule of the admiralty.

My grandfather, an affectionate, kind, peaceable man with light blue eyes and a soft blond goatee who sang 'Cherry blossom time' in an emotional voice broken by emphysemia, had spent all his active life on war ships. His cutlass is still up in the attic and his heavy camphor-wood trunk with its thick brass-bound corners and the identity disk with his name engraved in black on yellow metal: Paul Canu.

A war orphan, his first years were spent in the salt flats at Cotentin, near La Haye-du-Puits, looking after the cows, reciting to himself short impromptu poems that he wrote for his own amusement. Entered early on in the sailing fleet, he had weathered Cape Horn several times, waited interminably for the trade winds, sailed up the Yellow River, seen action in the China War, the Annam and Tonkin campaigns. He had returned with glorious multi-coloured medals, the rank of petty officer writer, bamboo ashtrays, the broken pieces of two translucent porcelain tea-services smashed on the way and a serious case of tuberculosis which caused his premature death. I only knew him when he was much weakened by illness but between coughing fits, always smiling.

I have the image of him stopping for a moment half way across the vegetable garden in his slippers, the backs of his hands resting on his hips; and then sitting at the round table in the kitchen, the leather elbows of his overcoat resting on the flowered oil cloth, meticulously peeling the small windfalls with his penknife to make stewed apples; or in the yard, just as patiently sorting and tying the shallots into bunches; the ones that had just been laid out to dry on old jute sacks in the autumn sun; or playing a game of *écarté* with my father in the dining-room, with the tame jackdaw perched on his shoulder playfully tipping his peaked cap over his eyes as he plays a trump; then grandfather would calmly straighten it with a gesture repeated a hundred times, muttering a long string of oaths under his breath. Sometimes, bored with that game, the daw—named Jack because of the call, imitating his own cry that my mother repeated in all directions to get him in at night—would suddenly jump onto the table, snatch a card in his beak and fly up to the top of the dresser where he would hide the card in between the pots of redcurrant and blackcurrant jam with brown paper lids, tied with thin pieces of string. A step ladder had to be fetched so that they could go on with the game.

Grandfather spoke little. I don't remember him ever telling stories about his many trips round the world, about which I know almost nothing apart from some bits and pieces reported by my mother or my aunts: the ship was away for three years...sheep and chickens were reared on board...when they embarked in Toulon the Breton sailors crossed the whole of France on foot...One day, Admiral Guépratte visited us in person to pin the Legion of Honour on the chest of the worthy servant of the Nation and its colonial empire. I was told it was a proud day for my grandfather. But I'm not sure now whether I was present at the scene or whether I was only told about it. Perhaps it was even before I was born.

And so that's all that's left of someone, after such a short time—and that goes for me too, soon, doubtless: odds and ends, frozen gestures, disconnected objects, questions in the empty air, a jumble of random snapshots with no real (logical) sequence. That's death...So, constructing a narrative would be a more or less conscious bid to outwit death. The entire system of the novel in the last century with its cumbersome machinery of continuity, linear chronology, causal sequences, non-contradiction was actually a last ditch attempt to forget the disintegrated state we were left in when God withdrew from our souls; an attempt at least to keep up appearances by replacing the incomprehensible explosion of atoms, black holes and impasses with a reassuring, clear, unequivocal constellation, woven so closely together that in the midst of the broken threads hurriedly knotted again we'd no longer hear death howling between the stitches. No objection to this grandiose, unnatural project...No objection, really? No objection to the Church? No objection to the Law? None, except that it's precisely the unacceptable acceptance of death itself: death of man, with a small 'm', in the name of some Ideal—capital 'I'—enthroned in the sky, death of each passing moment (I hardly have time to say: how beautiful you are) your death reader, that is, mine too. Artfully set up as realistic, this reassuring narrative—spurious (since it speaks in the name of an eternal truth)—totalitarian (since it doesn't leave room for any empty space whatsoever, nor for any plenitude outside the plot)—this blood-sucking narrative while claiming to save me from my approaching death, is from the start going to convince me that I've already stopped living, definitively.

Isn't the famous past definite tense, the 'past historic'—that's of no use in life and yet is the rule in that kind of novel— merely the sudden, definitive glaciation of the most incomplete gestures, the most ephemeral thoughts, the most ambiguous dreams, sense left hanging in the air, tenuous desires, stray or inadmissible memories? The 'simple' past is merely as simple—as certain and solid—as the tomb. A last flicker of life breathed into this hollow sham could now only find expression in the senseless art of representing oneself and the world as if cast in the same dense, imperishable concrete for all eternity.

Certainly, during the years I was learning to create a form of writing in search of itself (it still is), what was important to me was Sartre's surprising transition from *La nausée* to *L'âge de raison*. From the opening pages of the so-called *Chemins de la liberté* the new-born, elusive freedom which had made Roquentin's body tremble and his mind reel is suddenly brought to a stand-still by a past historic which comes crashing down on the characters (and the author ?) like a ton of bricks: 'Mathieu thought ...' Mathieu can think what he likes—that he's old, free, a swine—but as soon as he does it in this grammatical tense all I've got is an oppressive reading: Mathieu thought he was dead. His very freedom, his most precious possession then becomes

27

just one more fatality, an accursed essence which instantly freezes in his veins, since it's as if it had been decided by a god outside the text: traditional narrative technique. We can well imagine François Mauriac's sigh of relief: 'So much for M. Jean-Paul Sartre and his freedom!'

What's the modern novel—called the *nouveau roman* (we shall soon see why) doing now? Once more it's a narrative in search of its own coherence. Once more it's the impossible ordering of disparate fragments whose blurred outlines don't fit together. And once more there's the desperate temptation to create a fabric as solid as bronze....Yes, but what happens in this fabric, the text, is that it has itself become battlefield and stake. Instead of advancing like some blind justice obeying a divine law, deliberately ignoring all the problems that the traditional novel disguises and denies (the present moment for instance), the text is determined on the contrary to expose publicly and stage accurately the multiple impossibilities with which it is contending and of which it is constructed. So that this internal conflict will soon become (from the Sixties onwards) the very subject of the book. Hence the complicated sequences, digressions, cuts and repetitions, aporia, blind alleys, shifts in perspective, various permutations, dislocations or inversions etc.

Faced with the absurd or academic—anyway useless—attempt to say who my grandfather was, I feel like Roquentin faced with the Marquis de Rollebon's lifeless, scattered remains. And like Roquentin on the last page of *La nausée,* I realise that there's only one decision to make: to write a novel which, of course, will not be *L'âge de raison* but *Un régicide* for example, or rather *Souvenirs du triangle d'or...*

But we haven't got to that point yet since through sheer perversity, I am still fumbling on with a realistic, biographical, representational venture. For most of the day grandfather would do crossword puzzles at the kitchen table or on the narrow flap of his writing desk. He also spent a long time sorting out little bits of paper from his nine drawers made of pale yellow wood with a black border ...Having written this last sentence I wanted to

28

check that detail (was the border black or only the knobs?) so I went down to the ground floor of the spartan home in Normandy where I've been working for fifteen years. There are only five little drawers behind the drop-flap which also looks like a drawer from the outside. What does it matter? Anyway, this piece of furniture is no longer in Brest where everything has changed, even the design of the old house which was rebuilt after the war and is now nothing like the old one from the Thirties...

And now there's more confusion as I'm copying out this passage a month later in my flat in Bleecker Street in New York and I remember two quite different desks: one from Kerangoff and one from Mesnil-au-Grain. Besides, a cabinet maker has recently restored one of them.

Faced with the world which was changing too fast for him Grandfather would say: 'It's good to grow old.' And yet as he was dying he murmured, sighing: 'I still had so many things left to do!' Today the echo of that 'still' brings a lump to my throat. He must have been worrying about the scraps of paper in his drawers, the small windfalls, the delicate pinky-orange skin peeling off the shallots. We never ever finish putting things in order.

I'm not sure; the phrase 'It's good to grow old' must have been my other, much older grandfather's: Ulysse Robbe-Grillet, my father's father, a retired teacher (in Arbois) whom we called Grandfather Robbe to distinguish him from the first; I don't remember anything about him except his bulky shape and big mustache from faded photos.

I really didn't know Grandfather Canu any better. But I do remember liking him. He, I am told, wasn't very interested in me. I had long curly hair like a girl and was good at wheedling. I would cry if I grazed my knees. I was afraid to cross the dark courtyard at night to get to the old fashioned outside lavatory, even though it was only ten metres away. I would never be a soldier, nor wield the heavy cutlass ...(Beware: double trap for the psychomachine!) Come to think of it, I don't think my gentle grandfather ever used it either.

One last image: I see him from behind standing at the gate in the wooden fence that bordered the road, the left half is open.

He's leaning his right elbow on the letter box fixed to the side that's closed. I think he's waiting for the postman.

Behind him is what we called the front garden (the kitchen garden was on the other side of the house), a minute landscape garden with miniature lawns, shrubs—deutzia, weigelia, rhododendrons—and robinia, bay palms or Japanese privet instead of tall trees, not forgetting the two statutory chameerops palms which survived the bombing, fires and demolition work. All this, planted from seed or cuttings by Perrier the coast guard, my grandmother's father, seemed to us to be gigantic.

In front of him is 'Kerangoff plain', a vast, unfenced training ground where marines occasionally played at war games, went on manoeuvres; the rest of the time the plain was deserted, left to us for our excursions and mushroom picking, not to mention the herd of sheep who kept the grass cropped and whose black droppings we collected for the rose bushes and potatoes.

Still further away there are the roads of Brest which you could see clearly from that height, from the mouth of the Elorn right up to the Brest Channel, in the foreground was the naval dockyard and the sheltered road protected by two long causeways; the yawning gap—one red light, one green—right opposite our house seemed to be a magnificent extension of the wicket garden gate and the three granite steps leading to the corridor, long since disappeared, that divided the ground floor of the house into two equal parts. The front door with its high rectangular judas, the glass covered by a very elaborate wrought iron grille is now, hardly changed, in New York, the city of crime and rape, at the beginning of *Projet pour une révolution* ...Forgive me Jean Ricardou.

And what's become of my grandfather with his pale eyes lost on the grey horizon, bounded on the other bank of the roadstead by the Crozon peninsular and Menez-Hom? Perhaps that's him, old King Boris, still accompanied by the muffled thuds which echo from floor to floor, cellar to attic, the man who is taking such pains to repair the fragment of veneer missing from his desk, before facing the firing squad with a smile of farewell. And

30

yet the rooks in the hundred year old leafless beech trees are without a doubt the ones from Mesnil.

A few years after his death we had the superb summer of 1940. I had just done brilliantly in my maths course at the Brest lycée. The fine fleet had left the roads at nightfall, never to return. On leaving, the naval engineers had set fire to the underground reservoirs which we then realised really did exist. The fuel oil burned for almost a week. Amidst the din of the explosions burning pitch poured out of the hills near the *Maison Blanche* drowning streams and meadows, while formidable columns of red flames and black smoke dropped back onto the garden in hot suffocating fumes, laden with thick, heavy soot like snowflakes with the acrid stench of a smoking paraffin lamp—the taste of defeat, along with the paradoxical sense of freedom you feel at the collapse of your own nation (Psych. trap to be continued...)

I described the sensation of awesome catastrophe and emptiness a few months later in my first prose work which came after three poems written that year. It was a long short story to be called *Comoedia,* written in a strict classical form for a competition for amateur writers organised by a weekly newspaper that came out at the beginning of the occupation. I never received a reply and I too have lost the text. As I remember, it was of no interest: a sketchy adolescent love story ending obscurely in ruin.

The setting for the flirtation was probably inspired by my maths class which was mixed, a fact which doubtless occupied my studious mind unconsciously during the school year. Anyway, my young hero, abandoned and disappointed, saw the failure of his love affair counterpointed by our military defeat and disarmament. He finally embarked on one of the old boats that carried a few reckless boys off on further adventures, attempting to reach the English coast. Actually not many went because of the deep rooted hatred between these two peoples with rival navys; this was still further exacerbated here by very recent resentment over the common debacle and felt strongly by my whole family. So, the amorous disappointment bore no similarity to my own personal history which was not obviously passionate, nor to the dramatic departure when the reservoirs went up in flames. Or maybe my own ghost is fleeing from Vesuvius in pursuit of an indifferent, haughty Gradiva.

On the fifth day of the catastrophe I saw my first German soldier. He came rattling along on a motorcycle and side-car, on the sunken lane which came up from the arsenal onto the Kerangoff plain. A second soldier huddles in the passenger space wearing the same heavy helmet that crushed the nape of his neck, pointing a machine gun in front of him. Their faces were tired and drawn, livid with dust. Exactly the same greenish, mineral colour as their far from spectacular machine; they went diagonally across the plain towards the cemetery at Recouvrance, jolting over the uneven ground, solitary, ridiculous: our conquerors...Today they can be seen again in *Le labyrinthe* in their archaic vehicle, dead tired, vanguard of the enemy army which besieges the captured city.

I left the house two months later to get back to Paris. The next time I saw it it was in ruins. Kerangoff plain no longer exists. The uneven, winding road has been replaced by a straight tarmac street and pavements, named after a field marshal in the previous war against Germany, the one my father won; his stories of heroism punctuating the interminable nightmare of mud haunted the Parisian half of my over imaginative childhood with a nebulous fear: (You'll be a soldier too). The house which my mother lovingly rebuilt, (this time in stone,) around the old staircase that had miraculously survived the bombing, disappears today, swallowed up by council estates and from the bedroom windows on the first floor you can no longer greet the old ocean with its crystal waves haloed in grey mist.

Meanwhile I'd gradually had to face my ambivalence towards this sea I'd at first thought I'd broken away from. In the end I am bound to it by the strongest of links: I felt I was being dragged inexorably into the dreams and darkness that disturb the depths under the apparent surface calm, and the far too joyful fury of the waves that break and drop back sparkling like fireworks. For the whole period of the occupation the German military command forbade access to the Brittany coast; in their eyes owning a family house was not sufficient reason to go there. Perhaps I needed the physical break, the cutting of the umbilical cord, the long separation for the metamorphosis to take place in my head.

I can also think of a possible intermediary: music, which may have been a decisive contributory factor, or at least acted as a significant catalyst. At that time I discovered Wagner and Debussy. The indefinite series of vague chords never coming to rest in a set tonality—never gaining a foothold—was like the tide rising wave after wave despite its deceptive ebb. I don't remember any sudden, dramatic revelation behind some pillar at the Opéra or in the Salle Pleyel but I know that from the beginning of the Forties I couldn't listen to *Pelléas* or *Tristan* without feeling instantly uplifted by the insidious, perilous surge of the sea, soon to be sucked reluctantly into the heart of an unknown, unstable, irrational liquid universe ready to engulf me; its ineffable face is the face of both death and desire: old tenacious illusion of our Western world from Plato to Hegel, even to Heidegger, permeating the whole Christian tradition too, for whom this world is merely an appearance beyond which is hidden another more 'real' world which will only be lived after the final, blissful death by drowning.

When I do begin writing a novel four years after the liberation, I'm certainly not working from this perspective; on the contrary, my writing is a reaction against the fatal temptation to take annihilation for ultimate bliss, loss of consciousness for illumination, despair for beauty of soul. In all my first books I even led the fight with such persuasive valour, strengthening my fortifications with some polemical articles on theory, that looking at the criticisms at that time—unfavourable or otherwise—it's hard to find the slightest trace of the monsters I was combating. There was of course Maurice Blanchot and there were a few more. But what about the others, all the others?

It's strange though that so many readers, not all of whom were lacking in sensitivity and intelligence, were so easily taken in. Today if I open *Le voyeur* or *La jalousie* what strikes me right away

33

is precisely the strenuous, unflagging effort made by the narrative voice, the traveller Mathias and the anonymous husband, as they struggle against the delirium lying in wait for them, which surfaces in many turns of phrase and more than once takes over a whole paragraph. Obviously (and the same goes for me too, alas, when I read others) it's extremely difficult to perceive the complexity of a writer's text whenever it's in the slightest bit devious. I make an exception of Roland Barthes, whom no one can trick. Grappling with his personal demons, he did his best to outwit them by searching for a 'writing degree zero' in which he's never believed. My so-called neutrality—mere protective clothing—came at just the right moment to fuel his discourse. And so I was dubbed an 'objective novelist', or worse still, one who was attempting to be objective but who, without an ounce of talent, merely succeeded in being dull.

By chance yesterday in the office that's been assigned to me for a few months at New York University, I came across a vigorously annotated copy of *Le voyeur,* left on the littered bookshelves by one of my predecessors who must have taught the book and hated it. Everytime a particularly obvious trap is set he falls right into it and triumphantly notes in the margin the mistake I've made in relation to my detestable system. How can this professor fail to see that Mathias, deliberately contradicting everything I might say about the decent use of grammatical tenses, undertakes to describe his days on the island in the third person and in the obviously suspect past historic; this should be all the more suspicious in that he suddenly sees himself at key points in the narrative thwarted by short passages in the present which seem to escape his control ... But good heavens, not mine! At least give me that. Mathias, or more accurately, the text that 'expresses' him—uses the traditional language of irrefutable truth precisely because he is hiding something: the gap in his timetable. Similarly, he gives a minute, geometrical description of the world around him, whose treachery he fears, *for the purpose* of neutralising it. Besides, the sea monster (who devours little girls) is above all present towards the end of the book, and almost instantly you realise that Mathias, on the point of vanishing, has just got out of his depth.

34

As for the absent narrator in *La jalousie,* he is himself the blind spot, as it were, in a text based on the things that his gaze desperately tries to put in order, to control in order to combat the conspiracy that constantly threatens to upset the tenuous fabric of his 'colonialism': the luxuriant tropical vegetation, the rapacious sexuality attributed to the Blacks, the fathomless gaze of his own wife and a whole parallel, indescribable universe made up of the noises surrounding the house. How is it that so little has been said about the part played by sound in this novel which it has been claimed is devoted to one single sense: sight? The reason must be at least in part, in the disconcerting technique of the 'empty centre' which was being developed in *Les gommes* and to which we'll have to come back.

But a more general question comes up, for the author this time. Why complicate the reading of a novel by so many pitfalls and snares? That is, why *must* the text be set with traps? And how do these traps work? What is this strange relation I have with my indispensable reader since I do my best to mislead and then baffle him? It's certainly not easy to answer, but I must try or we won't be able to go on.

Actually I am hounded on all sides: why don't you say things more simply, why aren't you more accessible to the public, why don't you make the effort to be more comprehensible, etc.? Anyway, these are absurd ways of formulating the problem. I write first of all against myself, we've already seen this, therefore against the public too. Make what more comprehensible? If I'm pursuing an enigma which appears to me to be a lack in my own meaningful continuity, how could I possibly give a full, unbroken account of it? How could I express such a paradoxical relation to the world and to my own being 'simply'; a relation in which everything is ambiguous, contradictory, fleeting?

'Articulated' language, I emphasise this again, is structured like our lucid consciousness, which is to say according to laws of sense. Consequently, it is incapable of rendering an external world—precisely because it is not us—nor can it give an account of the restless ghosts within us. But at the same time I do have to use this lucid consciousness—and nothing else—which shows up the lack and the non-sense.

I've already pointed out how the modern novel chooses to take this (basic) contradiction not as a subject of study but as the organising principle of fiction. Let's take this further now. Bringing a fundamental lack into play in this way through the very structure of the narrative will immediately frustrate the reader, lure him in, then disappoint him, show him his place in the text while simultaneously excluding him from it, decoy him, using baits whose mechanics will be all the more complex since their purpose is not to produce anything: no external object, no feeling; all they have to do is 'function' like a peculiarly transparent multipurpose trap: trap for a humanist reading, for a political Marxist or Freudian reading etc., and finally, trap for the enthusiast of structures with no meaning.

This is where Mallarmé's *Sonnet en x* meets Marcel Duchamp's *Grand verre* which isn't made to grind chocolate—external object—nor to crush the dark bachelor demons. Actually what has just been said about written fiction applies to all the other constructions of contemporary art, although they aren't dependent on articulated language—from Jasper Johns' pictures to the silent theatrical performances of Bob Wilson or Richard Foreman. The same applies *a fortiori* to the cinema, since it is an acknowledged medium of fiction. But perhaps words are, after all, still the privileged means of expressing an experience of the void—since they are more shocking in the eyes of the law.

Is this, Oh Socrates! what people call gratuitousness? Let's examine this opinion, inherited from Sainte Beuve. To begin with we must be wary of people who use the word 'gratuitous' as an insult. When I read in a paper that in such and such a film there are gratuitous tracking shots I know that this only means that people can't see their precise 'significance'. Gratuitousness according to this consumer ideology is apparently defined in opposition to the 'excess yield' of meaning; actually that's not far wrong. And yet ...

And yet, can't people see that I myself am constantly attempting to justify myself—as I am once again in these pages? Because I too have this ideological relation to meaning (to the law), the thirst to encompass sense, an anxiety to supply it—of course I do. No, the *Grand verre* is not gratuitous, nor is the *Sonnet en x;* if they were, they would yet again be on the side of sacrosanct simplicity and not restless research. Hence the increasing complications in my own constructions, with *Topologie d'une cité fantôme* and *Projet pour une révolution* where anyone, by the way, could have spotted the famous bride stripped bare ... But let's not get ahead of ourselves, as King Menelaus would say.

So, in 1948 I decide to write a novel, on the spur of the moment. I leave the *Institut national de la statistique* where I already had a career marked out for me, and retreat to my sister's in Bois-Baudran, Seine-et-Marne, to a biology laboratory in the depths of the country, a centre for artificial insemination and research into hormones. My daily work—forty minutes, three times a day approximately—consists in taking vaginal smears every eight hours from hundreds of sterile rats who have been injected with urine from mares in foal and whose follicle stimulating hormone is then recorded, the stimulation threshold of each animal having previously been gauged by standard testing solutions. The rest of the time is spent writing *Un régicide* on the back of the pedigrees of the Dutch bulls whose sperm we sell to the peasants. First I write down the title and then the quotation from Kirkegaard about the seducer who 'goes through life leaving no trace behind'; the paradox is stated in these first words in the form of a self-contradictory object: the supreme crime that simultaneously effaces its own inscription. And the sea appears, my own double wiping out my foot prints; then I write my opening sentence, eternal repetition of an action that's always already been done, accomplished, without ever leaving a trace behind me: 'Once again, at nightfall on the sea shore, a stretch of fine sand, broken up by rocks and hollows has to be negotiated, sometimes with water up to the waist. The sea is rising ...' Insidious perils, fear, are keeping their appointment, as usual.

I'm absolutely sure that this opening is directly inspired by a recurrent nightmare I had for months on end when I was an adolescent. A few pages later, the hero of the book, Boris the regicide (in that text it's the king who's called Jean, onomastic situation reversed after nine novels in *Souvenirs du triangle d'or*), Boris the bachelor, Boris the dreamer is grappling with deepseated feelings of hopelessness, incapacity, bewilderment which he tries at once to pinpoint, describe and get rid of, which comes to the same thing. Here again childhood anxieties are rising to the surface, just when the ghosts of my sexual deviation have reappeared in my life, in a more imperious manner this time. Of course I'd been living with them for a long time, fifteen years, but now I have to accept the fact that only 'perverse' scenes (or fantasies) excite me: this is all the more problematic since I am especially attracted to very young girls.

In this first novel the ocean and its uncertain shores appear in a narrative in the first person present. The reader catches glimpses of them as if drifting through a dream (in which the plethora of metaphors almost drowns the 'poetry' of the grey heathlands and the fog); a dream that breaks up and soon distorts a 'realist' continuity written in the third person past historic. Boris works in a huge factory which I have no difficulty recognising as the Maschinenfabrik-Augsburg-Nürnberg (M.A.N.) where I myself learned to work as a lathe operator during the war.

The enormous machine shop with its seemingly endless rows of automatic lathes and milling machines lined up as far as the eye could see in a bluish spray of oily emulsion smelling of burning oil; warehouses, their blind walls built of small grimy bricks; the imposing entrance gate opening onto the long straight suburban avenue where ancient tram cars rattle along towards the distant cemetery in the South (we took the tram—as they called it in Brest—at the main station where, from dawn onwards we got off trains covered in coal dust, packed with passengers who were more or less deportees, sleeping on two-tier bunks in wooden barracks forming vast camps in the middle of the neighbouring pine forests;) also the clocking-in machines, the wall cabinets with our cards, the metallic passes to be shown at every check point—this whole scene, hardly changed, is the scene of my life in Nuremberg. On a joist in the roof above me was this harsh slogan, (painted in huge letters) which also applied to the German workers: *'Du bist eine Nummer und diese Nummer ist nul'* (You are a number and that number is zero).

Maybe, at first my regicide was rebelling against this unaccept-able law: the surest way to be recognised as an individual is to commit the heinous political crime of killing the king. Although Boris in his factory has a job more like my next one— statistician—in this first book the sinister face of the established order comes from my German experience; and today I realise this is no mere coincidence. Disintegration— the inconceivable horror at the heart of what had been the popular ideal proclaimed by national socialism (work, fatherland, sport, social laws, the cult of nature, blond adolescents marching along singing, a smile on their faces, bright-eyed and innocent, the soul as pure as the body according to the most reassuring imagery of cheerful good health—I think the brutal inversion of all these signs which suddenly revealed their other face had a more profound effect on me than the defeat of our own army five years earlier.

Of course my experience of these two successive breakdowns was very different, but it isn't exactly in good taste to admit it. The defeat of 1940 was certainly the defeat of liberty but my family would say it was rather the overthrow of levity, licence, negligence and a weak, pleasure-seeking mentality, in a word, the end of the Third Republic. The collapse of the Third Reich was, on the contrary, the collapse of a particular idea of order that might have appeared awe inspiring, the failure of a rigorous order that had become totalitarian, a collapse into blood and madness. I have mentioned that my parents were right wing, I must explain this more fully.

According to the official version of the truth which in other climes sends historians off to die in penal servitude, those whose evil genius impells them to ask how the battleship *Aurore* could fire on the Winter Palace when it wasn't in Leningrad in those glorious October days, whereas we are shown it well and truly moored at the quay on the Neva facing the Palace just where it should be, freshly painted every year (the truth has to be touched up regularly or it'll get patchy); according then to the official discourse, France at first appeared—at the Liberation—as a nation of heros pitted against the occupation forces from the armistice onwards in a quasi unanimous resistance; a somewhat untenable position which could, nevertheless, be maintained for more than ten years without provoking outright laughter or too violent a protest. Then comes a complete turn around: France was nothing but a pack of cowards and traitors who sold its souls and the whole of the Jewish people for a single crust of black bread.

I'm not going to venture a third version (I'm not a historian, thank goodness). But I must make it clear at this point in my modest autobiography that my experience hardly corresponds to either of those images. Let there be no misunderstanding: it's merely a question of saying, of trying to say, how I saw things around me; or even more subjectively, how I imagine today that I saw things then.

I was a good son, the very opposite of a rebel, fitting in at home where as soon as I got back I would recount in detail everything I'd seen and done at school or on the way; as for values, I had no trouble agreeing with most of my parents' political or moral options: it's wicked to tell lies, take the world as you find it, don't cheat in exams, the Popular Front is leading France to wrack and ruin, if you work hard your material and spiritual welfare will be assured etc., or even 'The richest aren't the poorest', since our folklore comprised numerous meaningless aphorisms, almost as a way of sending up those we did believe in.

I probably didn't have an unquestioning, unreserved admiration for my good parents, but I did feel a sort of sacred alliance with them, a fraternal community, a staunch solidarity. My father, mother, sister and I formed a sort of clan. For more than fifteen years I even wore a ring as a talisman, made of four intertwined aluminium bands that I'd picked up in a box of spare parts at the M.A.N. factory in 1943. Such family loyalty inevitably resulted in a certain alienation from the rest of mankind: a vague feeling of superiority, or at least difference.

One day at my primary school in the Rue Boulard, I had proudly replied to a school mate who was boasting about the captain's stripes his father had won in the forces, that mine was a lieutenant-colonel. When I got home I asked for some more information about the military hierarchy. In fact a pupil of the *Arts et Métiers* in Cluny, my father in a spirit of anarchy had

40

refused the additional military training which would have enabled him to serve as an officer. Mobilised on leaving school in August 1914 and sent to the front as an ordinary soldier, after four years in action his war had ended in hospital 'with serious facial injuries', with a Military Medal, *Croix de guerre* with bar and mention in dispatches, but only with the rank of second lieutenant.

Anti-militarism has certainly been one of the constants in his impassioned existence—curious right wing man who would show his children, not without a certain pride, the remark in red on his report from the *Arts* (where at the beginning of this century they still wore uniform and had close cropped hair) 'Affects a singularly untidy and slovenly appearance.' And so, that evening sitting round the family table where he invariably had his garlic sausage and white coffee, I learned that he was only a second lieutenant as an engineer with the French occupation troops in the re-possessed factories in Lorraine, but that if I wanted to, I could give him the five stripes of a colonel or the simple insignia of a sergeant, since these things were of no importance. Such was the clan's pride that it had no need of stripes.

The only war spoils he'd brought back were the complete works of Schiller—a large tome bound in grey canvas, printed in Gothic type of course—and a German signal flare, a sort of enormous pistol with a spectacular hammer, almost as heavy as a gun, with a short barrel as thick as my child's arm. This impressive trophy was hung out of reach on the wall of the room we called 'the study' which was used as the children's room. We were forbidden to play with this harmless weapon except as a special favour since you could easily crush a finger under the hammer if you were careless when handling the well-oiled breech.

After his evening coffee father would sit at the desk (a piece of furniture like a chest of drawers, from the American stocks) and enthusiastically translate Schiller's plays, one after the other, conscientiously covering squared exercise books with minute writing in indelible pencil. I think it was a sort of literal yet quite free translation since this zealous amateur didn't use his dictionary as often as he might, and most of the grammar must have been beyond him. Guessing, improvising, not bothered if his text didn't make sense or sounded strange he progressed quite quickly, unconcerned about other peoples' opinion. Anne-Lise my sister, whom we used to call Nanette, claims that it was one of the traumas of her youth (as when she realised a few years before that there was no Father Christmas) when she discovered that our father didn't know a word of German, that he hadn't learnt it at school or anywhere else.

Were we poor? It's obviously relative. Anyway, as a child I never felt in the least bit poor; I never thought of comparing such and such a school mate's flat (after primary school I won a scholarship to the Lycée Buffon, and my sister was a scholarship pupil too at the Lycée Victor-Duruy), or the flat of one of my mother's few friends, (like the close friend who was a dentist in Brest) with the three cramped rooms in the Rue Gassendi where all four of us were still living when I was over twenty; we didn't have carpets or chandeliers and the three bare bulbs hanging from the ceiling on little brass rings seemed perfectly normal to me, as did the sofa bed which was unfolded at night to change the dining-room into a bedroom after my sister—modesty forbids—stopped sleeping in the same room as myself.

My father, thanks to his soldier's pension, didn't make use of his engineering diploma from the *Arts et Métiers* to go into some metallurgical business; instead he joined a brother-in-law, who was a bit better off, to found the *Societé Industrielle du Cartonnage*, a pompous trade name for a minute cardboard box factory for mass produced dolls. Three or four workers assembled the boxes, my uncle delivered them, but my father had the hardest job: all day long he put the large sheets of brownish cardboard through the circular guillotine—a dangerous job which should have been done by a qualified worker; sadly the cost of the wages was incompatible with the prospective and ever uncertain business profits.

On Saturday nights, sitting at his desk which had been cleared of Schiller for once, my worried father initialled with a huge, illegible, superb flourish never ending bundles of bills of exchange which were repeatedly brought forward, many of which—I found out later—were purely and simply accomodation bills. I have since realised that throughout our entire childhood he lived in a state of permanent anxiety about this endless book-keeping. And I can still see his finger tips, strangely smooth and red, so worn from being rubbed by the cardboard in the cold winters (the workshop wasn't heated), with open cuts that took weeks to heal.

But on Sunday mornings he re-soled the family shoes, singing tunes from operettas, freely rendering words and music. He had all kinds of tools piled up in the cramped kitchen including a child's work bench; Father Christmas had left it for me in front of our parents' black marble fireplace where the toys on the twenty-fifth of December always appeared— this time it certainly was much larger than the chimney—I still use it occasionally in my more spacious home in Mesnil. Watching my father at work I developed a taste for manual work, from joinery to reinforced concrete and I'm sorry that I no longer have enough time to restore all the masonry, door frames, loose iron fittings in the property I love.

When the shoes were repaired father took us for long walks in the Spring along the fortifications towards Montrouge which was almost like being in the country. There was new grass, lilac round the huts and in the most desolate places bright yellow coltsfoot grew up through the whitish clay (the big leaves that came later were dried and used as a tobacco substitute during the occupation). We would come home about four in the afternoon for lunch which mother had cooked while we were out; we invariably had, one week in two, roast chicken or leg of lamb with *frites* and salad. The lovely smell permeated the whole flat. We were hungry. Night fell swiftly, mauvish grey outside, and the electric light on the round table around which the clan was gathered shed a warm orange glow and we would tell mother about our day's adventures.

I have nothing but happy memories of those Sundays that children are usually supposed to hate. And yet I think back on them without nostalgia: I don't feel that my way of life, my relations with the world, have changed fundamentally; as for the present narrative that I'm working on day after day, against myself, I wonder if it's that different from the painstaking, in accurate, absurd translation of Schiller's complete works. For dessert father would read us (rather badly) particularly polemical, vitriolic extracts, often including obscene jokes against republican institutions and their official representatives, taken from recent articles by Daudet and Maurras. I don't know what the extreme right-wing press is like today, but I do remember *Action française* in the Thirties as a well written exuberant paper, much given to Greco-Latin culture. The most violently offensive attacks were usually couched in the language of Cicero.

From my two left-wing grandfathers, staunch republicans of a confirmed yet good humoured secular turn of mind, partisans of Dreyfus, always ready to denounce the sinister union of the Army and the Church, my parents had retained an almost visceral atheism. The pernicious part on every level played by the Roman church was as little to be doubted as the fundamental incompetence of the generals. The excommunication of *Action française,* engineered it was said by Aristide Briand (nicknamed from then on 'the blessed pimp') upset many Christians, but for us was merely additional proof of the justice of the cause. Advocates of State Catholicism (for the people) yet excommunicated by the pope, monarchists yet disowned by the pretender to the throne, the *A.F.* leaders perfectly suited this family who liked nothing better than to feel they were different. Contempt for the self-righteous, a horror of the herd instinct (the *servum pecus*), plus the ludicrous series of parliamentary coalitions—all this lead naturally to a pronounced hatred of democracy.

After the ritual Sunday meal father would have a sleep or go and play a game of manille with the Jura cousins, concierges in Belleville. And then there were the special Sundays. When the large canal in Versailles was frozen over, we would skate on the ice lit by the winter sunlight. Sticking to the old country custom we had detachable skates fixed onto heavy walking shoes by a system of clamps. We took the train. We had knitted scarves wrapped round our necks. At nightfall on our way back we bought bags of hot chestnuts roasted on street corners on a big black iron furnace enveloped in fragrant blue smoke. This was a great joy. One night when it had been snowing a lot, father

44

on a sudden impulse even made us rudimentary (straight) skis out of small planks and leather straps to take us next morning to glide over the slopes in the Montsouris park...And then it's night once more, and the lights come on in the peaceful dusk frozen in the frost.

These sensations associated with night falling early in the winter city, or just after the beginning of term towards the end of autumn when the lights are already coming on earlier in the shabby shop windows of the neighbourhood bakeries or grocers, while it's still fairly mild and a fine drizzle sprinkles gleaming light onto the unevenly paved streets, and charcoal grey pavements where the last decaying leaves from the plane trees cling, musky and glistening ...I've often mentioned these very vivid (yet peaceful) sensations of evening calm, welcoming lamps, the distant hum of the city, vegetable soup, the lampshade covered with scorched paper as possibly the main reasons that impelled me to write a novel. I know exactly what it means to take up writing, having noticed the yellow of an old wall. Faced with the aggressive harshness of a book like *La jalousie* do my readers have the right to be surprised at such a confession? I think not.

They're extremely intense, unforgettable impressions yet nebulous, fleeting, evoked by the sticky (often comforting) adjectivity of the familiar world, by its emotional pressure which soon becomes unbearable, by its questionable insistence—they compel us to describe it in order to explore it or give it shape. But certainly with no intention of reproducing that adjectivity. Quite the contrary, in my own case. And yet any sensitive reader would have no trouble recognising in the 'childhood memories' of Wallas, the troubled hero of *Les gommes,* or in the two plaintive notes borrowed by the New York fire brigade from the Parisian one in *Project pour une révolution,* the faint echo of such poignant emotions ...

Now that I've taken up the present narrative again in the October of 1983 (as I indicated in the two pages added at the beginning of this volume) in the middle of the vast, foreign, rugged plains of Alberta, Edmonton, a city of luxurious modern skyscrapers totally different from the old neighbourhood between the Montparnasse cemetery and the Porte d'Orléans, I read over those lines about my family life around 1930 and am again amazed. Once more I wonder what these evocations mean. Why spend so much time recounting these more or less pointless anecdotes? When they do seem at all meaningful to me I instantly blame myself for choosing them (putting them together, fabricating them maybe) precisely in order to give them a meaning. On the other hand, if they're merely stray fragments that have come adrift, whose potential significance I myself may be looking for, why did I only pick these out of the hundreds and thousands which come up at random?

I'm caught in a bind: either I'm elucidating prefabricated meanings, or, on the other hand, exploiting the gratuitousness of a purely random pointillism (illusory into the bargain) as I grope my way forward at the mercy of obvious or absurd associations. If only I could hope to rediscover as I go along (by what miracle?) a few of the key moments that have formed me. But are there such things? And here the idea of a hierarchy, of classification comes up again. 'Tell me how you classify', Barthes proposed, 'and I'll tell you who you are'. So would a refusal to classify then constitute a refusal to be, a willingness merely to exist. Then why write?

Of course a considerable filial affection appears in my clan hagiography, like a small bouquet left on a grave. My father and mother lived mainly for their children; the best part of their work, worries, plans involved us. Isn't this a poor return in comparison? Am I not merely sketching a picturesque father, and doesn't everyone seem picturesque when painted? Can we accept that the entire life of a man leaves only these meagre traces, forgotten at the back of some drawer with a few yellowing photos of his irregular features, his big moustache, his puttees?

They are probably still there: the thousands of letters he wrote to my mother every day, over more than fifty years—love letters—even when there was a postal strike, whenever they were apart (for instance when she was in Brest with us for the summer holidays). There must be bundles of them in chronological order

46

lying at the bottom of some worm-eaten trunk in the loft in Kerangoff. Even at the time they were hard to decipher, doubtless they too will crumble into dust as soon as they're disturbed.

As for the obvious pleasure it gave me such a short time ago to say that our father wasn't left wing, it seems that this is rapidly turning out to be less scandalous than I thought. Who could this shock today? Now that the 'socialists' are in power in France, all wrong headed intellectuals will soon find themselves back on the right after a short period of purgatorial silence.

Another problem arises from the fact that I'm also talking about myself; or even solely about myself, as usual. My parents— that's already me taking shape. For whoever's interested I affirm my objection to the autobiography that claims to assemble a whole life (as if it could ever be water-tight) making it into a closed book with no gaps, like the old field marshals who put in order their ancient battles (won at a cost, or lost) for future generations. Now this downward path, this precipice I'm so close to is a constant threat. An awareness of the dangers isn't sufficient proof against the temptation.

In the Museum of Modern Art in New York, there's been a huge canvas on show for some weeks where I can be seen (as the title confirms) surrounded by scattered fragments. The young artist (whose name has slipped my mind)[2] has painted me kneeling in the middle of a sort of vast desert strewn with pieces of rubble that I'm in the process of cleaning one by one with a dust pan and brush. If you look more closely you can see that they're in fact perfectly recognisable objects, although they're fossilised, smashed to pieces; they are the wreckage of our civilisation, culture and history, such as the sphinx at Giza, Frankenstein's face or an infantry man from the first world war, mixed up with disjointed fragments of my own writings, novels or films (for example Françoise Brion in *L'immortelle*) and even my own

---

2. The American figurative painter of the New School is called Marc Tansey and the picture referred to: *Robbe-Grillet cleansing everything in sight*. (Editor's note).

face and a miniature version of me on my knees cleaning, turned to stone like everything else.

I recognise myself in this very witty allegory with pleasure. But having carefully cleaned the pieces am I not now artfully putting them in order? Perhaps even sticking them back together again to shape a destiny, a statue, the little boy's terrors and joys forming a solid basis for the themes or techniques of the future writer.

Putting things in order. Once and for all! The old naïve obsession resurfaces here and there, ironic, insistent, hopeless throughout my entire work as a novelist where the many sided hero never stops going over his daily routine with its flimsy framework, counts his banana trees over and over again, conscientiously masters his anguish or goes over the same episode again and again (hoping each time to arrive at a logical, rational conclusion), for example the precise account of what he's seen and done at the *Villa Bleue* on the evening in question. We must also note the minor characters who are partly conscious of this senseless obstinacy, for instance Garinati the clumsy murderer lining up the objects on his mantelpiece, Lady Ava trying one last time to put her papers in order before she dies, or the prisoner in the *Triangle d'or* who 'to vindicate himself' of goodness knows what crime, undertakes an exhaustive description of the bare walls of his cell.

Soon after the manuscript of *Les gommes* was accepted by the Editions de Minuit, having spent the modest sum scrupulously saved during my far too brief stay in the colonies, I'd found a convenient little job in Paris thanks to my qualifications as an agronomist and thanks to the help of Jean Piel who was then inspector general of the *Economie nationale*, George Bataille's brother-in-law and *de facto* director of the prestigious review *Critique*, in which my first jottings were published. So I was working at the *Assemblée permanente des présidents de chambres d'agriculture*, Rue Scribe, where I shared a huge office with two colleagues who must have been legal experts. My table was adjoining that of a remarkably thin, severe man who sat opposite. He looked at me over the files and heaps of documents that I tried in vain to pile up as a screen with the silent disapproval of the just man who has at first sight detected an impostor.

He was only there for a week or a bit longer and yet I have retained a surprisingly clear, solid image of this phantom judge with whom I hadn't exchanged ten sentences. He must have been seriously ill, was certainly aware of it and knew he was going to die. One morning when he arrived he began to take an inventory of the contents of his drawers. I saw him for three whole days, always silent, two metres away from me, sorting out masses of business letters, technical documents, memoranda of meetings, rough drafts, tables of figures, press cuttings and various odd bits of paper, re-reading, tearing them up, annotating them for his successors and classifying in carefully labelled folders everything he thought ought to survive him. Then he left his office punctually. He went into hospital that same evening for a hopeless operation and died the next day on the operating table.

I had read his condemnation of me in his dark ringed, sunken eyes which were already remote—their mournful glitter seemed to come from very far away: from the other side of the grave I thought later with no exaggeration. Of course he had instantly realised I was correcting the proofs of a novel and not articles on agricultural economy. He had seen my mind was elsewhere, that I too was merely passing through. I was a fake office employee. I had indeed been at the *Agro* (he had had to check it in a university calendar) but I was a fake agronomist. Although I didn't know it at the time, I was already a fake when I worked at the *Institut des fruits et légumes* where I'd gone to do research after finishing *Un régicide,* three years before.

A regional manager, who lived on another island in the Antilles, had visited me in Fort-de-France while on an inspection tour; he had shown me the report published by one of our research establishments in Africa. I therefore conscientiously studied what had been done, the experimental methods, the meticulous account of problems that had arisen, the columns of measurements and the reservations about how the statistics could be used, etc. The next day I pointed out to my superior that as all this research led to no concrete result whatsoever the

49

reports might just as well be considered as imaginative exercises. I quite seriously offered to write in a few days, entirely on my own, using several pseudonyms if necessary, a monthly report exactly like these ...

He took me seriously too. But a few months later, I was in hospital in Guadeloupe with multiple tropical diseases verified by all kinds of examinations and tests and this honest upright man not lacking in shrewdness, whom I think did like me and could appreciate the qualities which, despite everything, I had given proof of professionally, unhesitatingly stated in his report to the head office in Paris, which was concerned about my health, that in his opinion everything in my case was 'in the mind'. An irrevocable judgement (yet probably not as unjust as I thought at the time) which can again be found seven years later in *La jalousie* concerning the colonial diseases undermining the health of the invisible Christine, my boss having lent some of his most obvious characteristics (including that phrase) to the character of Franck, the neighbouring planter who always comes to dine without his excessively delicate wife.

In the last stage of his life Roland Barthes (him again), seemed obsessed with the idea that he was merely an impostor: that he had spoken of everything, from Marxism to linguistics, without really knowing anything. Already, many years before, I'd thought he was unduly affected by the criticisms of Picard who vigorously denounced his misreading of the 'real' Racine and his times. And yet Barthes had made it clear that all he was doing in his *Racine* was offering a contemporary reading which was therefore subjective, risky and precisely contexted. But he was suddenly chilled by the angry frown emanating from the old Sorbonne and felt a complex mixture of hatred and dread. And so later, feeling his age, he became more and more troubled about the possible existence—which he suspected—of real seventeenth century scholars, real teachers, real semiologists.

In vain I retorted that of course he was an impostor precisely because he was a real 'author' (and not a 'writer', to use his own distinction) and that an author's 'truth' can only exist, if at all, in the accumulation, excess and transcendance of his necessary lies. He would give his inimitable smile: a blend of unpretentious intelligence and friendship, but there was a certain distance, an absence from the world which was growing more and more pronounced. He wasn't convinced: he told me that I certainly had the right to be an impostor, that it was even my duty, but not his, since he wasn't a creator. He was wrong. It's his work as an author that will last. The semi-disrepute into which many people would like to see him fall so soon after his death is merely the result of a misunderstanding: the role of 'thinker' that was foist upon him.

Was Barthes a thinker? The question immediately raises another: what *is* a thinker today? Not so very long ago a thinker had to provide his fellow citizens with certainties, or at least with some rigid, consistent, inflexible straight lines to underpin his own discourse and so guide the minds of his readers and the consciousness of his time. A thinker is an intellectual guru. He was above all certain, this was his essential characteristic, his official brief.

Roland Barthes was a fluid thinker. After his inaugural address to the Collège de France, I was expressing enthusiasm for his accomplished performance when a strange young girl turned on me, passionate and angry: 'What are you admiring? He hasn't said a thing from start to finish!' That wasn't quite accurate; he had indeed been saying something, yet avoided pinning this 'something' down: using the method he'd been perfecting for many years, he withdrew from what he was saying as he went along. Deliberately undermining his provocative statement that all speech is fascist, which had caused such a furore that evening, he gave a disturbing demonstration of a discourse which was not: a discourse which destroyed, step by step, any temptation to be dogmatic. What I admired in this voice that had just kept us in suspense for two whole hours was precisely that it left my freedom intact—better still: at each twist and turn of phrase, it gave me new strength.

Dogmatism is nothing but the serene discourse of truth (complacent solid, unequivocal). The traditional thinker was a man of truth, yet a short time ago he could still believe in all good faith that the reign of truth was advancing hand in hand—same goal same battles, same enemies— with the progress of human liberty. On the façade of a solid Neo-Greek monument in the University of Halifax, Nova Scotia you can see: 'Truth guarantees your liberty'; and the headed notepaper from Edmonton that I was using this autumn has the following lofty motto: '*Quaecumque vera.*' Beautiful utopia, beautiful cheat that illuminated the euphoric dawn of our bourgeois society, and one century later the dawn of scientific socialism. Alas, today we know where that science leads. Truth, in the final analysis, has only ever served oppression. Anyway, too many hopes, wretched disappointments and blood soaked paradises teach us to be wary of it.

The preceding lines and those that follow originally formed part of an article that I was asked to write for the *Nouvel Observateur* on the anniversary of Barthes' death; so, it was just before the presidential election in the Spring of 1981. At this point in my text I made a joke—today unseasonable and somewhat bitter— which I shall nevertheless copy down: 'I shall vote for the Socialist party candidate since he at least hasn't got a manifesto.'

Unfortunately we then saw the candidate in question, who'd become our monarch, on the contrary take very seriously promises which many of his friends had until then only seen as vague speculations for the electoral campaign, the abstract ideas of the opposition which would need to be completely revised when they were eventually put into practice. Nothing of the sort has happened: premature nationalisation that has been needlessly disastrous, and even the dictatorial, uniform reduction of weekly working hours, opposed by the unions themselves; the Left's victory resulted instantly in a flood of short-sighted measures carried out in defiance of circumstances (as well as in defiance of the most experienced advisers) and solely justified, we are told, by the fact that they were 'in the manifesto'.

Certainly in all the decisions of principle that weren't made in the National interest nor in the interest of the people, the pledges that had to be given to the Communist allies must have weighed heavily—these allies, not the least of whose defects is obviously that they—they at least—believe in truth, that is, in the absolute and definitive value of what has been considered right once and for all sixty or more years ago. In any case we have once more been able to gauge on this occasion how pernicious a manifesto can be as soon as it's taken as law.

And even if the problems of human liberty are not exactly the same for running a government and for the lawless pursuit of literature, (which assuredly lacks sanctions,) there could still perhaps be an art common to these two disparate areas: the ability to contradict themselves in order to move on. As for me, I shall never side with those who reproach our president for having, a few months later, altered course, as it were changed tack, right in the middle of the storm he had unleashed. On the contrary, I like to think that such a daring manoeuvre shows that there is still some flexibility at the heart of this nascent socialism, the over respectful heir of far too aged traditions. It is said that on the day of his fatal accident Roland Barthes had lunched with François Mitterand. Do let's hope that on leaving he convinced him of the radical virtues of pulling back, of re-examination, of continuous change.

For, slippery as an eel (I'm talking about Barthes again), his shifts are not simply the result of chance, nor do they come from a weakness in judgement or character flaw. 'Messages' that change, branch off, veer in other directions—this is what he teaches. So, it follows that our last 'real' thinker will be the one who preceded him: Jean-Paul Sartre. He still wanted to enclose the world in a total (totalitarian?) system worthy of Spinoza and Hegel. But, at the same time Sartre was already possessed by the modern idea of liberty and that's, thank goodness, what undermined all his endeavours. So his grand constructions—novels, criticism or pure philosophy—have remained one after the other unfinished, open on all sides.

From Sartre's point of view his work is a failure. However, it's this failure that interests and excites us today. Wanting to be the last philosopher, the last thinker in terms of totality he ends up being a pioneer of the new structures of thought:

uncertainty, mobility, the breaking of new ground. And we can now see that the statement of 'useless passion' at the end of *L'être et le néant* wasn't so very different from Jean Paulhan's 'Consider this unsaid', though they appeared to be poles apart.

In 1950 Barthes enters this intellectual arena, which already seems to be in ruins. He is initially, strangely, drawn to the reassuring work of Marx. In a quarrel with Albert Camus over *La peste* he silenced the liberal humanist with the supremacy of 'historical materialism', as if it were some absolute value. But soon, gradually, he withdrew from Marxism, without a fuss, quietly as always.

He was once more lured into great systems of thought: psychoanalysis, linguistics, semiology. Hardly had the new label of semiologist had time to stick before he detested it. Openly ridiculing 'our three policemen: Marx, Freud, Saussure', he ended up denouncing the intolerable imperialism of all rigid systems in his famous apologue of the chip pan: a 'valid' system of thought that is too coherent is like boiling oil: whatever you put into it, you'll always get chips.

And yet Barthes' work is not a disavowal because of the constantly renewed movement of the self outwards, this movement that constitutes freedom (that could never become an institution since it only exists at the moment of its own birth); this is precisely what he had been pursuing passionately from the outset, from Brecht to Bataille, from Racine to Proust to the *nouveau roman*, from dialectics to his analysis of fashion. And like Sartre before him Barthes discovers very soon that the novel or the theatre—more so than the essay—are the natural setting in which concrete freedom can be most violently and effectively acted out. Fiction is like philosophy's 'world of becoming'. Was Roland Barthes in his turn a novelist? The question instantly gives rise to another: what is a novel today?

Paradoxically, in the 1950s, using my own novels as booby traps in his own terrorist activities, he would attempt to reduce their cunning dislocations, their implicit phantoms, their autoerasures, their gaps, to a universe of things which would merely affirm its own objective, literal solidity. Of course that aspect was present in my books (and in my theoretical writings), but as one of two irreconcilable poles of a contradiction. Barthes chooses to ignore completely the monsters lurking in the shadows of the hyper-realist picture. And when the ghost and spectres in *L'année dernière à Marienbad* invade the screen all too visibly, he beats a retreat.

I think he himself was grappling with analogous contradictions. He refused to see the spectre of *Oedipus Rex* or the obsession with sexual crime in *Les gommes* or *Le voyeur* because, struggling with his own demons he only needed my writing for its cleansing function. As a good terrorist he had only chosen one angle of the text, the most obviously acute so he could use it in the cut and thrust. But in the evening, when he came down from the barricades, he would go home to wallow joyfully in Zola's rich prose thickened with adjectives ...even if he were later to find fault with the thin sprinkling of adjectives in my *Labyrinthe*. Finally, ten years on when *Projet pour une révolution à New York* appeared, he recovered his enthusiasm and praised it as a perfect, yet 'mobile' 'Leibnizian model'.

None of this answers the important question: what novels would he himself have written? He talked about this more and more in public and in private. I don't know whether there are any rough drafts or fragments among his papers. In any case, I'm sure they wouldn't be like *Les gommes* or *Projet*. He would say that he could only write 'real novels' and he spoke of his problems with the past historic and the characters' proper names. Shifting even more dramatically than before it seemed that the literary landscape around him had slid back to the end of the nineteenth century ...After all, why not? The meaning of any research must not be defined *a priori*. And Barthes was subtle and devious enough to transform this so-called 'real' novel once more into something new, baffling, unrecognisable.

Henri de Corinthe, at least his memory, seems (has always seemed?) even more elusive, more difficult to grasp and often even suspect. Was he an impostor too, although of a different kind? Many of the people who knew him think so today, particularly those whose information and images are drawn solely from the gutter press. Anyway, it has to be admitted that his activities in Buenos Aires and Uruguay at the end of the Second World War and afterwards during the next ten years are open to a multiplicity of interpretations. Trafficking in shady merchandise, girls, drugs, small arms—(I must more or less consciously have used him as a model for Edouard Manneret in *La maison de rendez-vous,* who has also—I think—borrowed the physique of Mallarmé at his work table, in the portrait by Manet)—dealing in pictures too, fakes or otherwise, high or low politics, espionage—all these may be valid hypotheses and are not necessarily incompatible. On the other hand, one may wonder why this superior officer who didn't seem to be in any particular danger, had left France in such a hurry when the Americans entered Paris.

When I was a child I thought that Corinthe was a companion of my father from the trenches. Their friendship, which was otherwise inexplicable, could only have begun in the glorious mud of Cote 108 and Eparges. I realised some time later that this was impossible. My father was twenty in 1914 and Henri de Corinthe, who was much younger, was certainly not old enough to take part in that war, not even as a volunteer on the eve of the armistice. My obstinate confusion about this important point was doubtless the result of the legendary aspect of this fabulous yet still recent battle which, as if to distinguish it in advance from all others past and future, was simply called 'The Great War' and had captured my imagination very early on.

Neither family stories, which were curiously underplayed (in order not to disturb our young minds unduly), nor the overrated books by people like Roland Dorgelès, nor the heavy albums published by *L'illustration* which we had in the Rue Gassendi, reverently bound in fawn coloured leather and embossed in gold in which countless photos taken (more or less) from life were indiscriminately mixed up with heroic prints in a realistic style, nor even the injury to his inner ear from which my father still suffered managed to draw these gun carriages, cavalcades, corpses, the everlastingly muddy ground, the barbed wire, the victory out of a past that was already too awesome, too formidable to belong to any domaine but that of myth. Didn't Henri de

56

Corinthe himself tower over the common herd like some legendary figure? His personal history, filled with grandeur, shrouded in disquieting mystery, instantly found its natural place in a setting so appropriate it seemed made for him.

It is in fact a quarter of a century later that he won fame in battle, as a cavalry officer. But there probably was something anachronistic about the futile, bloody charge at the head of his cavalry in June 1940, against the German armoured divisions. So I can only imagine the sacrificed squadron as an old fashioned yellowing sepia print in *L'illustration*. Lieutenant Colonel Corinthe (who anyway was only a commanding officer at the time of the German attack) is charging on his white horse, his sword drawn in the midst of the standards; curiously he's looking towards the rear, doubtless to encourage his horsemen whose gawdy uniforms and glittering helmets with their streaming plumes are more reminiscent of some parade of the republican guard.

But in the foreground on the far left of the picture, almost under the hooves of the nearest horses, one of whom is even about to trample over his body, is a wounded man, or rather—it is to be feared—a dying man. Half-lying, the man is trying to raise himself on one elbow while his other arm—the right one— stretches forward both in the direction of his commanding officer and towards the smoke from the nearby enemy guns. There's no sword in his outstretched hand now and howls of pain not war cries must be coming from his open mouth. And yet the lips under his fine pointed moustache, the sweep of his arm, the very features of the soldier lying in the flower strewn grass in June and even the expression in his eyes—all these details are identical to those we are drawn to in the centre of the composition: the handsome, resplendent officer on his white mount, its nostrils flaring. And at times it seems to me that the latter is looking down at the dragoon who has fallen to the ground as if to bid farewell to his mortally wounded comrade, his double, his own life.

It is not particularly surprising that a few years later, this same Corinthe could be cast as a traitor, then—in really confusing circumstances—as an assassin. An assassin or a traitor doesn't necessarily lack courage. More disturbing certainly is the hypothesis that his military feats were indeed faked and, more precisely that they are those of a school friend who disappeared without trace in the turmoil. Similar things are said about his courageous deeds in the Resistance which are all the more difficult to verify in that they took place at a particularly confused time and place and the rare survivors are hardly willing today to talk about what they were doing at the liberation of the region, an episode which they are extremely reticent about. But if, as some people say, Comte Henri did usurp the credit and glory of a real hero, this is even more contemptible since this time it may very well have had something to do with his disappearance.

It seems it's this Corinthe who inspired my split protagonist Boris Varissa/Jean Robin in the film *L'homme qui ment,* for which I've often cited three more literary sources: the traditional Don Juan, the usurping Tsar Godunov from Pushkin and Moussorgski and K. the ostensible land surveyor who attempts to beleaguer the castle in Kafka's novel.

Don Juan is the man who has chosen his own word—daring, capricious and contradictory—as the unique foundation of his own—human—truth, a truth that can only exist in the present moment, as against God's truth which is by definition eternal. The moment—that's liberty. Don Juan knows this in his bones. And society condemns him precisely for being a libertine. He loves young women because they listen to him and so flesh-out his discourse; it is they who finally create his tenuous reality. His killing of the father is like the killing of the king, that is, the ideological law claiming to be God's law. A father willing to listen to him would straightaway cease to be the father. 'There's no such thing as a good father' Sartre used to write; through self hatred and hatred for his entire race he deliberately yet misguidedly confused papa, the good angel of the home with the pope, the guardian angel of dogma.

Boris Godunov is the false father, the murderer. He had the last son of Ivan the Terrible, Tsarevitch Dimitri whom he was supposed to protect, put to death in order to take his place as Tsar. He then reigns as absolute monarch. But he will be pursued

58

throughout his life by a double incarnation of retribution whose presence leads him inexorably to madness and death: first, the ghost of the murdered child who *returns* to demand reparation for the crime (God's truth, that's society's truth, can never be definitively abolished); and then on the other hand, the more solid shape of a new impostor, Grigori the monk, who passes in the eyes of the credulous masses for Ivan's last son miraculously resurrected from the tomb. This impostor posing as Dimitri, having gained the favours of the local princess in Poland, recruits an army of malcontents and ambitious men, soon joined by all the wretches in the empire. The last words Boris will utter as he dies in a fit of delirium are: 'I am ...still ...Tsar!' This is also the final cry of another mad emperor, Albert Camus' Caligula, as he falls under the knives of the conspirators: 'I am still alive!' That's also doubtless what the wounded dragoon in the picture was howling before disappearing into the mud of Reichenfels under the hooves of the maddened horses of his hundred and twenty comrades-in-arms.

K's relations with the law are, as we know, more complex: he pretends to be more naive, innocent as it were, when he's simply more devious. At first he pretends he's been called (as surveyor, why not) whereas obviously nobody asked anything from him. Then he's surprised that he's not welcomed with more ceremony. He complains, argues, negotiates. Like his brother Joseph in *The Trial*, he readily seduces the young girls he meets whom he hopes to make his allies. He's undeterred when rebuffed. Gradually he creeps into all the back roads that can lead him to his goal, getting nearer and nearer to the forbidden door which he knows very well cannot be entered, except by a corpse (who has, in one blow, lost his freedom). He always plays the victim when it's he himself who is persecuting the 'castle'.

His strategy is guided by a sort of instinctive knowledge of everything connected with the law. This isn't surprising: he is not opposed by the law. He is the law and the criminal. His paradoxical, obstinate, unreasonable—though seemingly reasonable—words, without which he would be nothing, are the very text of the book. *L'Homme qui ment*, despite fairly enthusiastic though obviously embarrassed criticism, was ignored by the public, doubtless because the avowed intention of the film was this time to construct narrative structures—in images and sounds—based on the generalised division of any sign into its inverse, as with the 'characters', the main part: Boris/Robin. So we're dealing with a story that's essentially elusive.

Now it is actually the film's internal structure that's the arena for all the conflicts previously described. Each element of the story—set, scene, piece of dialogue, object—is as if undermined by an internal split and the suspicion that it can only reappear elsewhere 're-turned,' in both senses of the word: returned and turned around. So, the whole story can only unfold through the cancellation of each thing into its opposite. However, Boris Varissa follows the ritual path: he speaks, corrects himself, goes on speaking, he imagines, he invents himself; thanks to his discourse he gradually insinuates himself into the hostile world of the castle, invades the girls' beds one after the other, grapples with the memory of the member of the Resistance who's disappeared, tries to appropriate for himself the veneration of which the other is the object and of course, ends up killing the father, believing he will be master in his place, for good. But he's reckoned without his own double, his shadow, this other with whom he wanted to change places, the so-called comrade in arms, the *real* hero, 'real' since his name is carved on the monument to the Resistance dead: Jean Robin. Boris is driven out like a pariah or a phantom, towards the forest from which he'd emerged right at the beginning (the *Urwald?*) whereas Jean returns without a word, secure as justice itself. And it's Jean the good son returned from the dead, the one who lost his liberty to the law, who will replace the dead father and reign over the gynaeceum that's been set to rights.

We are told that the traditional conflict that relentlessly pits the always wicked father against the inevitably wicked son—right from his earliest childhood—is the origin of all subsequent rebellion against the law. However, I have already stated that I've never felt murderous impulses against or even any sort of rivalry with the man who begot me, nourished me, whose name

60

I bear. Never *consciously* will be the unhesitating reply of the guardians of psychoanalytical order. 'Consciously: be damned!' I've even consciously felt quite the opposite. Of course our doctors have rejected this disclaimer in advance. But the refusal to accept any disclaimer is the principle flaw in all closed systems that don't allow for gaps, deviation or disagreement.

I believe I chose the career of biologist and agronomist for myself. Still, as I wasn't a child much given to questioning, my father could very well have chosen for me at the time, without my knowing, as the family got on so well together. Anyway, this certainly wasn't the case with my career as a writer. When I took the sudden, scarcely justifiable decision to leave the *Institut national de statistique et des études économiques* (where I'd been collaborating for three years with six other engineers from the top colleges, helping with the editing and reputation of the magazine founded by Alfred Sauvy *Etudes et conjuncture*) and launched into a novel (*Un régicide*) which I hadn't written a word of, I would normally have incurred various paternal reproaches. Nothing of the sort happened: the abrupt interruption of a promising career didn't raise any obstacles or remonstrance from my parents, and I was still living in the very modest family home. And, although this first novel was refused by Gallimard (a judgement which, at the time, could be taken as reliable) when a few years later I repeated my offence, leaving the *Institut des fruits et agrumes coloniaux* to devote myself entirely to writing *Les gommes,* again everything went smoothly: I was left free without the slightest reservation or expression of displeasure.

And yet they would have had the right to deplore—if even *sotto voce*—the long and costly scientific studies that they had allowed me to complete. There was never any question of it. On the contrary, my father made every possible effort to smooth my way, negotiating with the landlord so that I could have a cheap, minute garret of my own, Rue Gassendi; it was too cramped even for a small table, but in this attic solitude I was able to write on my lap three successive novels and I lived there until my marriage in October 1957. My father also offered to go on feeding me, three floors below, in return for a nominal sum.

And yet, in his eyes writing offered no reasonable hope of social success, nor would the life of a recluse be rewarded by fame, still less did he think of it as a possible way of earning a living. Things were a bit different with my mother who in her youth had been attracted to literature and had tried her hand at writing stories and poetry. Not so for my father. And my decision probably worried him, but since literature was my choice, albeit a late one, he now found his own justification— and despite everything, pleasure—in doing everything he could to enable me to devote myself to it freely.

An almost plausible explanation comes to mind: he was a *good* father because he was *mad*. Mother had always quite seriously maintained that father was slightly deranged, even suffering from recognisable mental disorders. She used to say that if I were intelligent it came from her side but if I were a genius (and of course she thought I was) it could only come from my father and, luckily, insanity had taken this fortunate turn. She always advised me not to have children for the same reasons (I followed her advice, not being particularly interested in babies, nor in little boys; little girls were another matter ...) She thought that my father's abnormal nervous condition was the result of being born of old parents and that he'd passed impaired chromosomes on to me. Her reading of *Le voyeur* soon reinforced her fears for my psychic and sexual health. It's a fine book, she told me when I'd given her the manuscript, but 'I would have preferred it not to be written by my son'. In a word, she was delighted that, in my case, potential infirmity had been transmuted into creativity; yet it was best to stop there: in her opinion there was a very strong likelihood that the next generation would produce monstrosities rather than eccentricities. Mother would say all this with the serene confidence with which she always expressed her decided, unconventional opinions.

She had a deep, solemn voice all the more persuasive in that she often spoke passionately. Then her tone was utterly positive: the unanswerable resolve of someone who knows. And she must have 'known' things, partly through her *reason* but also perhaps because of her very Breton sensitivity to *omens*. For example, several dozen years in advance she had announced the precise date of her death which was engraved with her initials—by an unknown hand—on the wooden base of her sewing machine, bought second hand from the American stocks just before her marriage. And now sometimes, at irregular intervals, I hear her voice again. It's usually in the evening before going to bed or falling asleep. But it can happen suddenly at any time of day. It usually lasts about ten seconds. The sentences are clear, very vivid, very near and perfectly articulated. And yet I don't know what she's saying. I only hear her tone of voice, the resonance, inflexions, the song as it were.

An image from the twenties in Kerangoff in the blazing mid-summer sun …Is it a story I was told a long time after? Anyway, I can see the scene clearly as if I'd been there. But how old was I? My father, on holiday, is stretched out on his back on a small path through the kitchen garden just under a hedge of gooseberry bushes and is trying to catch the ripe fruit in his mouth at the end of the laden, flexible branches which droop almost to the ground. From time to time he begins to bellow like a wounded beast. Is it because of the long thorns that make his task impossible or merely a sudden fit of despair? Grandmother Canu, scandalised, asked her daughter to put a stop to this incongruous din which'll disturb the neighbours and ruin our reputation for miles around. My mother, not taking the thing to heart, answers that with a husband like that she might as well get used to some eccentricity or strange behaviour. And she adds: 'I'd like to see you in my shoes!' 'My poor daughter', protests my grandmother with dignity, 'You wouldn't catch me making a mistake like that!'

At other times we did actually witness more worrying crises, although they were short-lived. At the Front my father was a sapper and had specialised in what was called mining, which must have been particularly appalling; he was still haunted by the memory ten years later. They dug underground tunnels, crudely shored up, through no-man's land beyond the front lines; then, crawling along even narrower tunnels six or seven metres underground they set mines under the enemy trenches. But the enemy was digging, in his turn under our tunnels, and so on, getting deeper and deeper all the time so that they never knew

63

which would be the first to be blown up. My father sometimes talked a little about the life of these men who were buried alive and about the muffled thuds of the German pickaxes throbbing in the soil as if coming from all sides at once, getting faster, stopping suddenly, starting up again louder, breaking the rhythm like a heart about to burst with anxiety—it was a matter of life and death—you had to estimate accurately the direction and distance in order to alter your own course. Staff sergeant Robbe-Grillet had been blown up several times, hence his repeated injuries...

In my early childhood my father would quite often wake up in the middle of the night, having a nightmare. He would leap up, ghostly, his cotton shirt floating around him, jump out of the sheets which were pushed back in a frenzy and run through the small flat, wild-eyed, yelling 'Put out the lamps!' My mother, still in her armchair at the table in the dining-room, calmly put down her paper, led my father back to bed and soon to sleep, talking soothingly as if to a delirious child (*'Siehst du, Vater, den Erlkönig nicht?'*) She would then turn to the frightened children and reassure them as best she could. He must have been shouting about the Davy lamps that had to be put out quickly before the explosion, I don't know why...Or was it the opposite: Did he shout 'Light the lamps!' I don't remember anymore.

My father himself readily admitted that he wasn't really normal. It didn't bother him in the least. He would say, half smiling: 'I've got a screw loose...' Not, he explained, because his parents were elderly when he was born, but because of the war and his head injuries. For many years he'd been pleading his case at the appropriate ministeries, and been referred for experts' reports in order to get himself officially recognised as 'insane'. To supplement his meagre pension as an ex-serviceman with head wounds, decorations, etc., he was loud in his demands for additional, much more substantial compensation for permanent insanity as a result of the cranial traumatisms suffered at the front: the shock of the explosions, shell splinters, etc. However, the experts weren't convinced, and the magistrates always dismissed his claim: maybe he was unhinged but the war could not be held responsible!

My father having a screw loose reminds me of another expression
current in the family, referring to a particular kind of anguish
or profound mental unease: 'My head's full of stripes', 'this
business gives me stripes in the head'...An expression that came
from one of Kipling's stories in *Traffics and Discoveries* where a
lighthouse keeper, lost in the treacherous waters between the
Sunda Islands, goes mad in his lighthouse. He constantly sees
stripes streaming over the surface of the sea below him, lines
of spindrift forming among the eddies and stretching out endlessly
in parallel lines drifting with the current. He blames this
unbearable phenomenon on the ships coming up the straits accus-
ing them of ruling lines, as it were, over his personal territory,
on the floor of his dwelling and ever inside his brain. He reacts
by sending out false signals in order to divert the traffic into other
passages and so stop the ships from continuing to disturb the
treacherous channel which he's watching over and with which
he identifies ...

In my childhood I spent hours watching the little streaks of
whitish spindrift tracing more or less regular patterns of parallel
curves on the deceptively calm flowing water, everything sliding
almost imperceptibly but always in the same direction between
the rocks at Brignogan, on that coast of granite and storms where
my grandmother's father, whom I never knew but whom the
family called grandfather Perrier, had in the past been a
coastguard. When we were very small my sister and I were taken
there from time to time on the miniature railway from Brest
which seemed like a toy, to spend a few days in an old fashioned
stone cottage with very thick walls, narrow windows, very spartan, built on the parapet walk by the shore and only separated
from it by a patch of garden washed at high tide by the spume
from the sea. It was 'Perrine's house' unless I'm getting
muddled—an old friend of the customs officer's two children—
Grandmother Canu and Godmother; they'd spent their entire
youth in the village with the little peasant girls and fishermen's
daughters, mainly speaking Breton, going in the evenings to sit
up with one or another to read the Lives of the Saints, then listen-
ing to the traditional tales of shipwrecks, ghosts and wandering

souls whom they then heard keening in the starless night as they went back home in their clogs along the sandy paths sodden with rain where, mingling with the gusts of the west wind, the unleashed hords of phantoms brushed against them.

Little streaks of whitish spindrift, sea swirling insidiously among the huge heaps of pink granite blocks, sand hollowed out at the foot of the rocks by the never ending almost invisible eddies, treacherous beaches and little waves whose regular motion was deceptively reassuring—all this aquatic universe, as seductive as it was dangerous, gave me bad dreams. They reappear in several of my *Instantanés* and also in the nocturnal anguish at the beginning of *Un régicide*. But the similarities between that novel and a short story by Kipling that I only noticed recently can't be coincidental. It's called 'The Best Story in the World.' A young office clerk is troubled by persistent recurrent visions, particularly clear and vivid ones that seem to belong to a previous life several hundreds of years ago, one or two thousand maybe, when he was a galley slave. The harsh orders of the slave master, the cracking of the whip, the rhythmic movement of the oars, the nostalgic songs of his fellow oarsmen and above all the huge wave which hangs suspended, towering over the gunwhale just before the shipwreck and which will break over the men chained to their benches...all these images burst in on him, more and more tangible and dramatic until the day of his marriage when everything stops abruptly, leaving no trace ...Sisyphus, Kafka said, was a bachelor.

Grandfather Perrier, Marcelin, Benoit, Marie, doubtless had the job of watching over a small sector of the coastal zone, but what for? Was there the chance of a bit of smuggling—tobacco, alcohol, materials, contreband from England? What I have heard about are wreckers who lit gorse fires on the cliffs to mislead foreign ships and lure them onto the reefs where they broke up, leaving scattered cargos and the remains of their shattered hulls to be pillaged. Yet most of those stories seem to come from earlier times or to be the stuff of legends. On the other hand, shipwrecks were common in these waters in bad weather and the coastguards had to allocate the wreckage washed ashore. So at Kerangoff there was a bedroom in solid mahogany which was Marcelin Perrier's, made for the wedding of his daughter Mathilde (my grandmother), with billets of rare woods that had been washed up onto the shores of his territory.

All the men of the family spent some time in the Navy and were then coastguards till they retired. In the attic (it was Grandfather Perrier who had had our large wattle and daub house built) I found the service records of the three last generations, written in the Spring of 1862 by François Perrier, my great great grandfather. Because I've always been moved by the laconic quality of this yellowed sheet of paper I'm copying it out here as it is, only adding punctuation. I think the text (rather than the piece of paper itself, which seems to have been copied out again by another hand) was written by François, Marcelin's father, because it contains more details about him, especially '*our* departure from Brest'—the first person must have slipped out despite his obvious concern to be objective.

'Perrier, called Va-de-bon-coeur. Aquitaine regiment, seventeen years. 1778 war. Four years in India under Bailly de Suffren. Discharged in Vannes, the barracks regimental depot, 1784. Coastguard Service, twenty six years. Died 20 Novembèr 1832.

'Perrier, François, Jean Marie, younger son of Benoit. Five years and six months serving the State, army and navy. Began serving on a gunboat of 21 guns on convoy service in the Channel, Captain Bozec, 11 January 1811. Discharged in May of the same year. Drafted to Brest for training until 17 August the same year, the day of our departure from Brest with a cadre of the 17th naval battalion, Captain Prateau. Left Boulogne with this battalion 22 March 1812 for Danzig in Prussia and then for the Russian campaign. Transferred to the bridge-train March 1813 at Mayence, after the retreat from Russia and fought on in the 1813 campaign in Saxony and Silesia. Taken prisoner in the aftermath of Leipzig under the walls of Targau in Bavaria and taken to Berlin in Prussia in October the same year. Escaped from prison in November and returned to France 13 December the same year to the fortress of Kehl. Sent to Brest with a travel warrant issued by the Strasbourg Naval Office and arrived 24

December the same year. Attached to sixteenth naval battalion at Brest, Captain Bijoux, from 14 January 1814 to October the same year. Recalled in March 1815 for the Vendee campaign in emergency artillery company, Captain Conseille, mustered out in October 1815. Saint Helena medal.

'Marcelin Benoit Marie Perrier, older son of François Jean Marie. Five years and six months in the navy on board the steam frigate *Asmodée*. Mustered out 15 May 1849 as quarter master, first class. Coastguard service, fifteen years until the present (15 April 1862).'

Marcelin had married Marie-Yvonne Magueur, whose brother died on active service at Toulon and whose father was in charge of the postal service in Finistere. For him, as for all these sailors, soldier or coastguards, serving the State was a sort of sacred mission as well as an honour. One day he hurled himself in the path of a procession which, to his mind, was moving too slowly. Cutting off a procession! In the first years of the nineteenth century, in Brittany! To the outraged man of God brandishing his cross to ward off evil and prevent sacrilege it was said that my ancestor Magueur had shouted majestically from his seat on high: 'God in heaven Father! The Mail must get through!' My family still cited this act of civic outrage in the face of the clergy's obscurantism and superstition.

Henri de Corinthe on his white horse, his head held high, sitting very upright as usual, refusing to slump in the saddle but clearly swaying to the left, a position he often adopts after a long tiring ride, Henri de Corinthe on a calm night of the full moon crosses the heather-clad country bordering a deserted cove in the jagged coastline of Léon. Just as the track he's following joins the narrow coastguard path beside the shore his ear, atuned to the sounds of the sea, picks up a louder noise coming from the direction of the water, mingling with the regular splashing of the waves of the ebbing tide; it's also rhythmic, yet sharper, stronger more distinct.

Tightening the reins very slightly he stops his horse to listen more carefully. It's like the repeated slapping of a vigorous paddle on wet washing. There is indeed a stream flowing into the beach in this spot, but who'd be washing in the moonlight away from all human habitation? Corinthe immediately thinks of the ancient peasant belief in 'nocturnal washerwomen': young women from the spirit world, harbingers of ill-fortune, rather like the witches in *Macbeth*. Smiling to himself he wonders if they're about to announce his imminent accession to the throne of Scotland. (The Corinthe family have distant ancestors in Wales and Northumberland, one of whom was the famous Lord Corynth who fought against Cromwell). Comte Henri approaches the minute fault hollowed out by the running water and follows it to the beach.

Just before he gets there the stream bed widens out to form a sort of small pool. It would, at a pinch, be a possible spot for washing and, lying sideways on the edge of the shimmering pool, there actually is one of those rough wooden boxes where country women kneel to beat their washing with a paddle. But the worn chest seems to be abandoned and there's no one in sight. Besides, although the noise is more and more distinct it seems to come from further away, as if from the sea itself. Well, the intrepid rider remarks inwardly, this nocturnal washerwoman doesn't seem to mind washing in salt water! And more intrigued than ever he spurs his horse across the strip of sand to the water's edge.

There's not a living soul here either, not in front of him or on either side; the sweeping curve, festooned with white spindrift is sparkling in the pale nocturnal light. The ground's fairly hard in this part of the bay so the horse's hooves aren't likely to sink in. Corinthe urges his beast towards the open sea, stepping into the shallows which only just come up to its knees. The odd slapping sound is now very close and soon, about twenty metres away, the man sees a flat object dancing on the crest of the waves, rising at each wave, then dropping back into the trough of the next and gleaming with an extraordinary light.

After a few more steps—more difficult because the horse is resisting—Corinthe realises it's a mirror, kept afloat by its thick oval frame, the upturned glass, depending on the angle, reflecting the moon's rays onto the rider. But when the latter wants to cross the few metres that still separate him from the piece of wreckage his faithful horse refuses to move. At first Corinthe thinks it's because of the waves which are now a bit rougher and at times come up to his chest. So he waits a few seconds to let him get used to them before spurring him gently forward.

Then the animal rears up terrified, and begins to jerk his neck violently, obviously trying to turn round, at the same time opening his mouth wide to get rid of the bit. The rider has to master this unusual, incomprehensible resistance. He's stimulated by the battle and all the more agitated since the coveted object is now moving away, doubtless dragged out by the ebbing tide. However, the mocking tap tap goes on, even more vigorously, beating a more aggressive rhythm, more vehement each time the oval mirror—which must be very heavy—drops back into the expanse of water.

Although there's hardly any wind the waves suddenly seem much bigger and rougher than is usual at low tide in this fairly sheltered cove. The horse is now maddened, his master can't hold him. An even larger wave having broken over them, the beast rearing up vertically, succeeds in unhorsing Comte Henri. Managing to regain his foothold in the icy waters, hopeless, he sees his mount, its nostrils flaring, turn round instantly and gallop towards dry land, neighing continuously, his head straining backwards like a wolf baying at the moon. Spindrift rises beneath his hooves and the spray mingles with his sparkling white windswept mane in a bluish light that suddenly flares up with the radiance of an apocalyptic vision.

However, Corinthe, although unhorsed, struggles desperately, sometimes swimming despite his heavy water-sodden clothes, sometimes wading when he regains his footing in the interval between two waves, then jerked out of his depth again, pulled under the heavy sea, losing his balance and breath for several seconds, stunned, tossed about, dragged further and further out by the receding piece of wreckage. But, in a last burst of energy he gains enough ground to manage—God knows how—to cling on to it. The object seems so heavy that Corinthe wonders by what miracle it's staying afloat. The exhausted man is afraid he'll never manage to bring it ashore, he feels as if he's carrying a dead weight. The oval frame is more than a metre high and

70

the carved wood is as solid as a ship's gunwale. Corinthe clings on with all his strength. He battles desperately against the tide pulling in the opposite direction, not noticing how long his struggle goes on …

Thanks to a superhuman effort he does succeed in accomplishing the absurd task he felt compelled to take on. He drags his prize out of the water and utterly exhausted drops onto the sand as if about to fall asleep on the spot. But he's trembling with cold, weariness and nerves. His muscles contract in a series of involuntary, painful spasms. And his mind's gone blank.

When he opens his eyes again he sees his white horse leaning over him with a look of sadness, anxiety or reproach. Comte Henri turns away, half raising himself on his elbow and looks at the mirror lying beside him among the scraps of seaweed and shells left by the ebbing tide. The huge carved frame seems to be made of jacaranda or some dark mahogany from South America. The glass itself is tarnished, doubtless from its pro-longed immersion in the sea, the surface is sprinkled with drops of water that are beginning to dry. But in the cloudy depths of the very thick glass whose glaucous tints are accentuated by the wan moonlight, Henri de Corinthe sees distinctly—and almost without surprise—the reflection of the gentle, fair face of his lost fiancée, Marie-Ange, who was drowned on a beach in the Atlantic near Montevideo and whose body has never been found. She is there in the mirror her pale blue eyes staring at him, a mysterious smile on her face.

A short while afterwards—a few minutes at the most—Corinthe must have lost consciousness. A coastguard from Brignogan on his morning rounds was astonished to find a solitary, magnificent white horse in the middle of the beach, a rich man's horse with its fine black leather saddle, and nickel stirrups sparkling despite the overcast sky, but the bridle is hanging from its neck. He therefore approached and immediately discovered the body lying in the sand beside a large oval mirror in a carved mahogany frame, such a deep red that at times it seemed like ebony.

Lying on his back the man looked like a corpse. The rising

71

waters, it's almost high tide at that hour, were lapping the rider's boots. But his clothes, which must certainly have been very elegant a few hours before, were already so soaked with water that the officer's first thought was that he had a drowned man on his hands, washed ashore by the sea. And yet the proximity of the horse, who could hardly have been shipwrecked on a sailing boat with his master (whose clothes perfectly matched the luxurious trappings of the animal) made this seem unlikely.

On the off chance, the conscientious officer wanted to take the usual measures to expel water from the lungs in case this really was an accident by drowning and there might still be time. The only result after a few moments of effort was that the eyes of the corpse opened; he was then seen to be very much alive, but so disturbed by goodness knows what adventure that remaining motionless, he was equally incapable of uttering a word. He didn't even seem to understand the pressing questions of the person in uniform who had just erupted into his dream and whom he stared at wild eyed as if desperately trying to come down to earth.

Meanwhile, having made sure that there was nothing broken in the solid, well built body the coastguard who, although small was uncommonly strong, succeeded without too much difficulty in getting the rider onto his feet. But there was no question of hoisting him onto his horse in his present state. So the best solution seemed to be to help the invalid up to a small bar at the end of the next cove (at Ker-an-Dû where a narrow tarmac track led to some fishermen's cottages) and wait for a doctor while the horse could carry the mirror which the officer was sure belonged to the stranger.

But when he cautiously made as if to put the heavy, fragile object on the saddle to which he hoped to fasten it with the reins, as best he could, the beast as if panic stricken (whereas until then he had been standing very quietly, if a little distance away) reared up on its hind legs winnying, then dropped back heavily, began to back away snorting violently through its nostrils, its four legs splayed, head lowered in such an extraordinary attitude that the customs officer himself took fright.

The mirror was too heavy for him to carry up to the inn, so

he decided to leave it there, merely putting it out of reach of the high tide at the top of the beach where he could have it fetched later by some seaweed gatherer's cart. Then he returned to Corinthe who had watched the whole scene without saying a word, impassive, still standing on the spot where he'd been left, yet staggering on his stiff legs and obviously in no fit state to take a step on his own.

While he was doing his best to support a considerable part of the weight of this tall, weak body leaning on his chest as they went on their hazardous way, tottering along the narrow, awkward path, the customs officer was now reflecting on the mirror's inexplicable presence on the beach. In fact, it wasn't very likely that this elegant horseman—however strong he may be—had been riding with such a heavy, cumbersome burden. Then maybe it was just a piece of wreckage thrown up onto the coast; and in that case it would belong to the Nation and not to the stranger who'd found it. Unless he'd swum into the sea and fished it out, which hardly seemed compatible with his outfit: why would he have worn clothing so unsuitable for such a dangerous undertaking? And any way, even if this were the case, wasn't he within his rights to claim a third of the prize for himself. All the same he could only claim this provided that no other heir or owner showed up within the time prescribed by the law.

There did, however, remain an even more disquieting possibility: that the three elements—horse, mirror and rider—were all together on the shore by pure chance, with no link between them at all, not of causality or ownership. While the men stagger on their hazardous path across the country with their arms round each other, followed three metres behind by the pensive horse, the excessively scrupulous guardian of public order progressively loses himself in the complications of maritime law and problematic hypotheses...

What happened next is, from this point on, much more obscure. It certainly does seem that Henri de Corinthe reached the hamlet in much better shape. Maybe the painful walk on the arm of his saviour had helped to revive him? Doubtless he didn't want to wait for the unpredictable arrival of a doctor; the coffee laced with alcohol which the innkeeper normally served to the seamen being enough to relieve his dazed condition. But it was also said that he had to be put to bed at the inn as soon as he arrived and was laid low by such a high fever that for several days there were even fears for his sanity.

In his delirium he murmured partially inaudible, incoherent, disjointed sentences in which a young woman who was dead was constantly mentioned; at moments it was thought that he had accidentally killed her himself, at other times that she had disappeared, shipwrecked in a boat equipped for under water hunting. One of the peculiarities of his story—which made it almost impossible to grasp—was that as well as being incoherent, full of contradictions, gaps and repetitions he kept switching from the past to the present tense yet seemed to be going over the same period of his life and the same events.

However, one thing was certain: the very day he made his dramatic entrance into the cramped, dark room in the bar at Ker-an-Dû where a small group of fishermen at the tables suddenly fell silent, turning round one after the other towards the open door through which he had just entered (in the firm grip of his uniformed keeper), Corinthe—mysteriously eluding all surveillance—supposedly returned on horseback to the scene of his nocturnal adventure, evidently intent on retrieving his formidable treasure. To conciliate the two apparently incompatible versions—his rapid recovery or his prolonged stay in bed—one can imagine that the sick man, not giving in to his fever but misleading his obviously anxious hosts about the real state of his health, had actually slipped away very early with some excuse and thanks to the reflexes of a seasoned horseman had managed to trot to the maleficent beach (considered as such in a whole series of legends and local superstitions, which I often heard in my childhood).

Although the final sequence of the episode (called 'the ghost in the mirror') still remains extremely confused, since accounts vary considerably and are mixed up with vague memories of folklore, there are a certain number of indisputable points we can use as guidelines. When Corinthe comes in sight of the

74

cove—which he remembered clearly—and anxiously glances round the curve from the top of the dunes covered with pink heather and clumps of sea-thrift, he realises at once that the mirror has disappeared. The tide is going out and a gently sloping wide silky strip of sand with an inviting hollow is already uncovered, forming a perfectly smooth fresh golden stretch where this morning, curiously, the ebb tide hasn't left any seaweed or other debris so that the smallest piece of wreckage would be visible at a glance.

Nor is there any trace of what the man on the horse is seeking at the foot of the dunes on the dry, ridged sand which the high tide didn't reach. The water in the bay is as smooth as a lake, and this rules out the possibility of a recent storm during which the raging sea could have swept away various objects left on the coast. On the contrary, the whole atmosphere is so peaceful that Corinthe, as if forgetting a bad dream, walks his white horse forward, the latter quite soothed too, when suddenly as he reaches the channel carved out by the stream in the sloping shore-line, he once more catches sight of the box left by a nocturnal washerwoman beside the translucent pool.

The wooden platform isn't in such a bad state as he'd thought in the deceptive moonlight. The oak is only bleached and worn from use. You would swear that someone has just this minute been using it. Three steps more and Corinthe discovers (and its just as if he'd come to this spot unconsciously seeking the thing, so strong is the feeling that he was expecting it) hanging on the higher branches of heather covering the other side of the hollow where the little stream flows, three articles of freshly washed feminine lingerie, drying in a sudden ray of sunlight— a thin, improbable beam of yellow light slanting down out of the grey sky.

Because of the delicate refinement of this silk finery with its enchanting, old-fashioned embroidery they couldn't possibly be the underclothes of a simple peasant girl. Aren't they actually ...Have Mercy! My God have Mercy! The torn chemisette, the small triangle, the lace—here is where the man on the horse remembers having ...Have Mercy! Have Mercy! On the small lace pants and the matching suspender belt there are large fresh blood stains that seem to be seeping through—scarlet, shining unbearably bright.

Then Henri de Corinthe felt a chill creeping rapidly through all his limbs, his chest, his whole body. And there's nothing strange in that if you think that he hadn't even changed his clothes since his prolonged immersion the night before. Doubtless it was this terrible chill that brought on a serious pulmonary disease; the enforced stay at the inn, the high fever and delirium all having a perfectly rational explanation.

But it's also said that the faithful horse with its blond mane had, from then on, been strange, skittish, difficult. Brignogan folk say that horses can't see their reflection in a mirror and that in the glaucous depths of the drowned mirror, rather than seeing the face of Marie-Ange the murdered fiancée who pursued his master, the white horse had for the first time seen his own image, his death. The firm belief that that night the animal changed into a sort of demon or spectre was strengthened in the eyes of the credulous peasants by the fact (which was, moreover, confirmed) that you could never hear the sound of his hooves, even when he was galloping over hard ground.

Still today no one doubts that the horse was bewitched, if only because of its lively grace and exceptional beauty, but on the other hand even the rough date of the incident of the mirror remains a mystery. The scene ought in principle to have taken place quite a long time before the defeat of 1940, many details that I remember attest to this: the still wild aspect of the North Finistère coast which has since been spoiled, the tradition of the coast guard's daily round along the cliff, even the officer's uniform, the dark old room in the Ker-an-Dû café etc.

Also we mustn't forget that Corinthe's injury from the front definitely stopped him from riding. Everyone remembers his stiff leg and silver-topped cane, that not only helped his balance and made his limp less noticeable but also gave him the gait of a dandy which he turned to his advantage, enhancing his elegance and prestige. Now Marie-Ange Van de Reeves, the young dead mistress, whose charming yet reproachful face unexpectedly reappeared in the phantom mirror, died while visiting Uruguay with Henri de Corinthe, who, we know for certain—didn't live in South America till after the end of the war. Had he had some love affair there before? It's unlikely. Didn't his intense political activity in the Thirties, given his connections, preclude the possibility of any improper honeymoon, crime or accident aside, even on the other side of the Atlantic, by the distant shores of La Plata?

But I sometimes think I'm confusing the fair Marie-Ange with another pretty girl, Angelica von Salomon who was also very close to the count. Perhaps I'm unconsciously giving Corinthe character traits, military feats or other more anodine biographical details that don't belong to him but are borrowed from other more or less famous personalities of the time: Henri de Kerillis, François de la Rocque or even the comte de Paris who was also called Henri and was a pretender to the throne of France.

In the beginning of the Thirties my father, like many ex-service-men disillusioned by their victory that had cost so dear, anxious patriots increasingly disenchanted by the parliamentary regime, had belonged to the *Association des Croix de feu*. But its founder Colonel de la Rocque, was subsequently suspected of using his troops on the 6th of February 1934 to protect the Palais-Bourbon in secret collusion with Daladier's police. The accusation, which I think came from *Action Française*, can't of course be verified but it illustrates perfectly the multiple divisions and sectarian quarrels that existed among the extreme right wing factions.

Beside it's only in 1936 or even in the beginning of the next year that Corinthe, disregarding the advice of his closest friends, officially founded his own group: *La renaissance socialiste nationale* (while in his youth he had been elected as a Deputy on a monar-chist ticket thanks to a short-lived experiment with full propor-tional representation). The movement had little success and was almost instantly forgotten; there were too many small parties with very similar aims arguing over the somewhat limited possibilities for action and also quite reticent in the face of the declamatory, aggressive and vacuous character of the manifestos. Today it is more with a sense of boredom than nostalgia, yet with some surprise, that I rediscover these more or less pro-fascist civic passions, disillusions, even bitterness echoed in the 'character' of Laura in my first novel *Le régicide*.

Corinthe's different political hats (didn't he also have a brief flirtation with the Communist party in one of the most Stalinist periods in its history?) were probably merely a way of expressing his own uncertainty and increasing anguish in the face of mounting danger. To die with panache in a futile battle against the armoured divisions of the enemy—who was precisely, through an ironic twist of fate the Germany whose spectacular recovery he admired and, to a degree at least, its ideology—was certainly a solution he had contemplated with equanimity. He had returned with a limp, albeit as elegant as ever, ready to throw himself wholeheartedly into the most dubious causes.

In his memoirs as a director of the Théâtre Français, David Samuelson says that just after his adolescence Corinthe dreamed of becoming a great actor and that he'd acted in public in small Parisian theatres, sometimes even playing major roles. He then showed a marked preference for historical dramas in which he played solitary heros with an imposing, gloomy destiny: Napoleon, Berlioz, Cromwell ...In this context Samuelson notes that every politician is a failed actor. The opposite could just as well be said.

Towards the end of the Thirties the financial situation in my father's cardboard box factory had gradually improved. As well as the summer holidays which we always spent in Kerangoff at our maternal grandmother's (and we then went to the sea for shorter periods, staying in a peasant's cottage that my mother's elder sister had converted near Quiberon), we'd begun to take short winter holidays too, in the Jura, this time with real skis and all the equipment we would lovingly get ready weeks in advance. (It was the time you used dubbin for the boots, bindings with adjustable straps, and Norwegian wax with tar—the strong smell of resin permeating the flat).

Since Grandfather Robbe's death we no longer went to Arbois where, when he was alive, we'd enjoyed the sensuousness of Autumn; gathering the windfalls and fresh nuts on the paths in the countryside as it turned to russet. (An enlarged, slightly blurred photograph with the château in the background surrounded by leafless trees shows me at seven or eight in a cotton apron like a little dress, encircling the flowering hollyhocks in my raised bare arm; my brown curly head is tilted towards them, I'm smiling winningly at the camera, graceful as a girl.)

But my father's brother—quite a bit older than he—was postmaster at Russey, near Morteau in the Doubs. It's there that we learnt to glide over the gentle sparsely snow-clad slopes in the clearings between the firs. We stayed at a small café-hotel for travelling salesmen which my uncle used to frequent. He was a debonnaire man, often a bit drunk, a Sunday painter in oils: winter landscapes—cottages and forests in the snow—not taken from life, since he didn't like to leave town, but copied from post-cards. His work was for sale exhibited among the crates of fruit and vegetables at the neighbourhood grocer's. The firs in his pictures looked like herring bones. He cheerfully agreed. Then joking and punning he would dwell on his disappointments as a misunderstood artist.

Anyway, the scenes that stick in our memory are usually the most insignificant, pointless ones: they stay in your head forever but you don't know what to do with them. Here's one which for no reason at all insists in being included in my story. I went back to visit this Uncle Maurice ten years later. He had retired to Ornans and as I remembered him as being a likeable man, I wanted to drop in unannounced while I was on a cycling trip from the Vosges to the Alps with Claude Ollier, whom I'd just met in the labour camps in Germany.

I had a great deal of trouble finding where the ex-postmaster lived because he called himself Robbe, having dropped half of his too complicated name which had, however, been in the family for at least a dozen generations. The place wasn't exactly a hovel but almost, as I thought at the time, and still do today—gloomy, dingy and delapidated. I have to climb up a rough wooden staircase with several treads missing or loose and just at the top there's a hole in the floor barely concealed by a bit of roofing felt. My uncle and aunt have been drinking as usual. The litre of red wine is still on the table among a pile of utensils that are difficult to identify. The whole room is so cluttered with miscellaneous objects I don't know where to put myself. At last Uncle Maurice recognises me, anyway he realises I'm his brother's son. Aunt Louise, in a drunken stupor is collapsed in a corner on such a low chair that I thought at first this fat, shapeless bundle with a red puffy face on top was lying on the ground. Every thirty seconds she repeats in the same peevish scared voice: 'Who's there Maurice?'

They both died soon after. My father went to the funeral (at Ornans, Oh Courbet!) and brought back a couple of things to remember them by: a small cherry-wood sofa with a curious flexible back from Arbois (it's now here in Mesnil) and two gold wedding rings found in a pin tray. I adopted them on my wedding day, never having known for whom they were made. The wider only fitted my right ring finger but there was no church nor priest to reproach me. So, I've been wearing it on that finger for more than a quarter of a century. It took the place of the four aluminium bands I mentioned earlier which had worn thin and brittle. The narrower was made even smaller and repolished for Catherine. As for Aunt Louise's anxious question, I'm quite sure it was the *formant* for: 'Maurice, don't shoot!' in *Les gommes*, when a police inspector made up a sordid version of Daniel Dupont's murder.

After two years we abandoned Russey for a tiny village in the Haut Jura which we visited regularly until the war; the mountains were much more picturesque and the skiing conditions were better. There was always lots of snow, sometimes too much. We were enchanted. 'Putting on your skis at the hotel door' seemed an undreamt of happiness. There were still no official ski slopes and you went up by tying skins to your boots, but there was a variety of suitable walks and coming down was easy. All four of us were happy there— or more often all three—since mother wasn't so strong. Alone in the world at nightfall in the white mountains that suddenly turned pink and blue as we came back in single file through the stretches of virgin snow bordered by the fir trees swaying under their new fur coats that the night frost would freeze solid; thin black silhouettes slowly advancing along the shelf, from a distance apparently motionless; father in his Alpine huntsmen's gear leading the way, followed one behind the other by his two children; happy too to see mother again and tell her of our feats and find the warm lights of the comfortable little hotel which was exactly on the frontier, with one door in the front in France and another at the back in Switzerland, which amused us immensely. (Our favourite rooms were the ones which were cut in half right down the middle by the theoretical line separating the two nations). Winter sports hotels have a very special smell when you come back to them from the cold air outside; its so unique that I won't even try and analyse it but I've felt the thrill again, afresh, many years later in Davos or Zermatt.

During all that period my mother was often ill (and we had to take this into account in the holidays as well as other times); in fact she had a classic fibroma but refused to have an operation, out of respect for nature she would explain, preferring to stay in bed for days on end reading her papers. My father was never in the least reluctant to do the daily shopping, washing up or other domestic chores. Since we were relatively better off financially, an invaluable, devoted family help—a formidable Swiss woman whose speech was corse and racy—took over the housekeeping and cooking; she made vast apple tarts and kept the extremely thin puff pastry a state secret (she would shut herself off to make it in the tiny kitchen and we could hear her loud exclamations accompanied by the sound of the rolling pin wielded as vigorously as a paddle destroying everything in sight); she actually ruled, as well as scoured the little flat in the Rue Gassendi where we now had a Moroccan carpet, frosted glass ceiling lights with brass in the style of the 1930s that's already coming back into fashion.

This good lady stayed with us a long time: before, during and after the war. But she always stormed in like a whirlwind. When she arrived in the early morning (we were still in bed sometimes) she would fling the windows wide open all over the flat even in

81

mid-Winter so the strongest possible drafts blew through the house. She then began to 'clean the pig sty' (piggery) which meant battling against our untidiness. In the midst of the ensuing storm with doors slamming and curtains flying she first hid anything left lying around, usually in the most unexpected places, saying that that would teach us to tidy our things away; then she would sweep so energetically that the wooden broom hit the walls and furniture which still bear the marks. Once, we found her in the dining-room standing on the side-board: she'd decided to clean the top with the steel-wool polisher usually used on the oak floor that also suffered in its less resilient parts.

When we got home at mid-day we couldn't ask what she'd cooked for us since she would invariably say that she'd made 'noddels' (at least that's how I imagined the spelling) and as, at first, we'd ask what that was she would answer with a loud, devastating laugh: 'Prunes in shit!' Then, possibly hoping to get us to share her enthusiasm, or merely to prolong the inexplicable joy her answer unfailingly gave her, she would immediately repeat it two or three times.

When war was declared all the debts from the cardboard box factory had finally been paid and my father decided to give up his share in the business to his only brother-in-law and take various administrative jobs, first in the Ministry of Supply then, after the armistice, in other similar kinds of organisations.

A little later, thanks to connections that he'd kept up in the doll manufacturing world, he went into the *Chambre syndicale des fabricants de jouets* where he became secretary general—just about the time I began writing. He enjoyed acting the part of an official, sending himself up as he played at being the important gentleman attending professional meetings, travelling abroad, meeting ministers; he showed off a bit when he wore a new suit, as he had in the past as the dashing Lieutenant Robbe-Grillet in his uniform at the Hagondage steelworks where Yvonne Canu, our future mother, was a shorthand typist.

My parents were obviously Pétainists, but unlike the usual kind they still were—maybe even more so—after the Liberation.

82

About 1955, I was at home entertaining my new writer friends, staunch leftists several of whom had been active in the Resistance. At that time my father had a passion for porridge: every evening he cooked his ration of grey gruel for his dinner—very tasty, as they say in Brittany—made with milk and slowly stirred with a wooden spoon and he willingly served large helpings to all the visitors. Michel Zéraffa, Jean Davignaud or Lucien Goldmann shared his ration and concealed their surprise on seeing a large photo of Pétain in khaki smiling above the sideboard (the one where the floor polisher had made a large hole to remove a tiny scratch) placed in the most prominent spot against the raffia wall paper. They politely averted their gaze, endeavouring not to see the shocking anachronism. But Duvignaud the sophisticated man of the world said one day between spoonfulls of porridge, as if it were merely an oversight: 'Ah, you've kept the Marshal's photo.' This one had in fact adorned nineteen out of twenty French homes for four years. 'No, not at all,' my father answered, 'I haven't kept it, I put it up on purpose the day the American troops entered Paris.'

And he had. Under the German occupation he hadn't seen any reason to advertise such a conformist, officially sanctioned veneration on our walls. But he already felt an unreserved affection and respect for the legitimate Head of State. For him Marshal Pétain was the soldier of 1914, the trenches, Verdun, the slow recovery of our armies at the time of the greatest despair and victory, finally. The signing of the armistice in 1940 was also credited to his wisdom and courage, whereas he had no part in the defeat. The historic handshake at Montoire demonstrated above all his integrity as a soldier. Curiously this professional soldier was, for the sake of the family cause, even credited with underlying anti-militarism. And we weren't going to lose any sleep over the scrapping of political parties, nor over defunct parliamentary debates! Out of loyalty to Pétain, as opposed to De Gaulle the wicked rebellious son, my father had even made a strict point of voting communist for several years, resolved to do this—he would say—until the ashes of the old Marshal were transferred to Douaumont to be placed beside his infantry men.

My parents were confirmed anglophobes, a position which certainly seems to contradict what I've said about English literature—for children or adults—that we'd been brought up on from our early childhood. But this was to a large extent due to the influence of one of my mother's girlhood friends who was a bookbinder in Paris, where she led a precarious existence, half Bohemian, half poverty stricken. This Henriette Olgiatti whose grandfather Magnus claimed to be a direct descendant of Charlemagne (she would tell us this with her sarcastic yet warm laugh which inevitably turned into interminable coughing fits), was of Jewish origin and much drawn to British culture. With her brilliant lively mind, cultured, speaking a very literary language easily and playfully she probably played a considerable part in forming our tastes, particularly in the vast, indefinable realm of humour. She spent a great deal of time at our house under any pretext, smoked two packets of Camels a day, bubbling over with anecdotes—if only about her own misfortunes—when she wasn't reading to us(*The Just-So Stories*, *The Water Babies*, or *Captain Corcoran*) and my father often had to throw her out late at night so that everyone could finally get some sleep.

So for us hatred of England was strictly political but it certainly didn't date from the last war. On the contrary, our common military reversals merely rekindled ancient animosities: throughout my childhood I'd been lulled to sleep with old sea shanties from *Primauguet* to *Trente et un du mois d'août* which are hardly flattering to our neighbours across the channel; it was with emotion that we were told about the fishermen forgotten on a little island at the tip of Brittany whom the police had come to fetch towards the end of the Summer of 1914 to announce, after some delay, the general mobilisation and who, without a moment's hesitation as to who their hereditary enemy was had shouted 'This time we'll stuff their arrogance down their throats—English swine!'—they were quite crestfallen afterwards when they realised their mistake.

The result of the fighting in the North in 1940, the evacuation of Dunkirk, ('Your lordships the English, save your bacon first!' was said in a tone of derision), then the destruction of our

84

defenceless fleet at Mers-el-Kébir where hundreds of Breton sailors died (the gravestones at the Recouvrance cemetery in the corner of our Kerangoff plain bear witness)—everything helped to rekindle age-old feelings of distrust, ever ready to break out into violent execration against 'Perfide Albion'—who returns the compliment.

Given the least opportunity this still happens today: the French people gloat on the quiet when a French built missile sinks a British warship in front of the isles we persist in calling the Malouines and if a referendem were taken, this treacherous ally would be speedily expelled from the Common Market since she really does appear only to have joined in order to scuttle it more effectively. (I am writing these lines at the end of March 1984.)

So, German propaganda was on very safe ground when it shamelessly exploited the rich vein of anglophobia in the French, calling willy nilly on Joan of Arc, and Cato the Elder (England, like Carthage...), even re-publishing Willette's cruel sketches or insulting pamphlets dating from the Boer War which my whole family, seething with anger, thoroughly enjoyed. The heroic resistance of our former partners in the Baedeker raids didn't count for anything in our eyes: as usual the English were defending their own interests not ours. And they only repulsed the overt or insidious pressures of certain more or less Germanophile American business milieu so energetically because they couldn't bear to see their eternal nightmare realised: a European federation. That the leader of the federation would be a madman called Hitler was merely in their eyes a minor consideration.

Maybe this was my parents' opinion too in a way since their nationalism didn't prevent them from having been long-term confirmed supporters of a united, not to say unified Europe (but without the English, heaven forbid!). So quoting with total conviction the saying attributed to a British statesman (Disraeli?) 'When I'm hesitating between two solutions I only have to decide which will do the most harm to France,' their position *vis-à-vis* a victorious Germany could only be more ambivalent. Prussian militarism and thirst for conquest was a danger of course, but on the other hand one day or another Europe must be created and include Germany (Nazi or not). The periodic wars on the

Rhine or Moselle were merely the perpetuation of a tragic mistake. Let's forget these frontier disputes between two nations who have the same interests at heart; they're as outdated as the disputes in the Middle Ages that tore apart the France of today...

Despite his rigid sense of honour, it wouldn't have taken much to persuade my father to find excuses for those (numerous?) soldiers in 1940 who hadn't wanted to fight. The war against Germany reminded him too vividly of four nightmare years: mud, cold, shrapnel, poison gas, enemy trenches cleaned out with bayonets, men dying with their entrails hanging out, howling for nights on end between the barbed wire—and all for nothing. Since we were unable to establish bonds of co-operation and friendship with Germany when we were the victors we had to try now as the losers.

Such a gamble certainly went hand in hand with an unshaken confidence in the destiny of France which, freed from the misguided ideas of a republican demagogy would soon find its soul again and end up imposing its genius alongside the complementary genius of its first cousins. After all, we had already been conquered by Rome: two peoples often have a great deal to gain when they unite their conflicting qualities.

My father and mother firmly believed in the Franco-German partnership as the centre of a future, larger confederation whereas as staunch supporters of Maurras they ought to have counted on our 'Latin sisters'. Previously at school they had made us learn German and not English as our second language since as gifted pupils we were studying classics. Later when my sister and I had to take a second language for the exams we chose Spanish.

However, after the defeat this 'collaborationist' spirit was never translated into action, not in the form of a commitment to a party, nor in any personal fraternisation with the occupying forces. The 'silence of the sea' was the rule for us too; it was a matter of dignity: a hand held out to the conqueror was not to be confused with an eagerness to lick his boots. But in a symbolic gesture my father had in a way buried the hatchet: when the *Kommandantur* ordered civilians to surrender their personal weapons he went, sick at heart I imagine, to throw the useless signal flare he'd brought back from the front into the sewer.

My parents were anti-Semitic and they freely admitted it to anyone who cared to listen (even to our Jewish friends, if they got the chance). I wouldn't wish to gloss over such an awkward point. Anti-Semitism still exists almost everywhere in various more or less insidious forms and is always likely to break out again and wreak havoc, like a fire left smouldering in a heap of embers that has been carelessly left unguarded. To fight successfully against such a widespread, tenacious ideology it is essential, firstly, not to make it into a taboo subject.

It seems to me that my family's anti-Semitism was a fairly common type: not militant (turning over a Jew to German or Vichy persecution would, naturally, have been abhorrent); nor religious (the god *they* had crucified was obviously not ours); nor contemptuous (like the Russians); nor obsessive (as in Céline); nor was it an antipathy either (Jews could be exciting to read or pleasant to know, like anyone else). Meanwhile, extremely irrational as in its more virulent forms, my parents' anti-Semitism seems to have been 'right wing', since it was obviously motivated by a basic concern for the maintenance of moral order plus a deep seated distrust of all internationalism.

Just as Communists are always suspected of working for the Soviet Union which they would cherish as their true native land, so the Jews were firstly, accused of belonging to a very powerful supranational community which was much more important to them than their French passports. With no real 'roots' in France they are allegedly bound spiritually and by their origins to another 'land' than ours and they themselves would always feel more or less stateless. International capitalism was an analogous category for which the term Judeo-plutocrats was used, as if there weren't many more poor Jews in the world than millionaires, and as if all arms dealers were Israelites.

Even more disturbing is the notion of the Jews sewing the seeds of moral dissolution. For not only were the Hebrew people in exile alien to our national essence but they were also considered to be immigrants of a particularly pernicious kind, creating from one end of old Europe to the other widespread uncertainty, the break down of conscience, domestic and political chaos, in brief, swiftly bringing about the ruin of all organised society, the death of all healthy nations.

Today, using a vocabulary that certainly wasn't ours at the time, I would say that Jews throughout the world could be seen as unique fermentors of liberty. Of course that too is merely a stereotype without which many noble Israelis and the majority of zealot rabbis would no longer have the right to be called Jews. However, if we stick to this imagery it's not just the morbid taste for misfortune, catastrophe and despair that is readily attributed to them (although at the same time they're accused of amassing fortunes at the expense of the social body whose parasites they are) that reminds me precisely of what Heidegger says of anguish: the price to be paid for achieving freedom of mind at last.

This is where for me the irreducible opposition between notions of order and liberty appears to be simplistically embodied in the two stereotyped portraits of the German and Jewish people. This explains the xenophobic sliding scale which excluded Jews from the community when they'd often been French for several generations, in order to attempt a union with the Germans who were at all events not yet French. But they at least were on the right side: the side of order.

To combat the formidable virus of contagious negation and metaphysical anguish (i.e liberty), my parents were certainly far from imagining any 'final solution'. They were perfectly satisfied with the 'reasonable' *numerus clausus* advocated by Maurras. Like many sincere people under the occupation we obviously didn't know that the Nazis were about to take quite different steps. Most of the Jews who were deported didn't themselves know. As for my mother, she always considered planned mass-extermination to be so inconceivable that she continued to deny the reality of genocide right up to her death in 1975. She saw it merely as a matter of Zionist propaganda and faked documents: people had also tried to convince us that the Germans were responsible for the systematic massacre of Polish officers discovered in the cemeteries at Katyn.

88

We found a culpable resignation in the face of (inevitable) misfortune, and habitual despair in all the fiction that we actually read avidly (especially my mother and I), in spite of the term 'Jewish literature' which we used to refer to it at home. I mention here a random selection of the books we blithely classified under this label, some of whose authors were certainly not Jewish. *Dusty Answer* by Rosamond Lehmann, *Tessa* by Margaret Kennedy, *Fortune carrée* by Kessel, Hardy's *Jude the Obscure* and also the great trilogy by Jacob Wassermann: *Der Fall Maurizius, Etzel Andergast, Joseph Kerkhoven*, or *Rebecca* by Daphne du Maurier. I think Louis-Ferdinand Céline was lucky enough to be officially recognised as a right wing anti-Semite, otherwise *Voyage* and *Mort à crédit*, which for me are still his two great books, would certainly have been tarred with the same brush; this would not however, have stopped us reading them over and over again with delight, quite the contrary ...

Yet having got to this point in my story I'm now finding it more and more difficult to go on saying 'we' when speaking of the family ideology. I wanted to mention Kafka's novels here and immediately realise that I didn't read them till after the war and then I had changed. Of course we never stay the same from one year to the next, one hour to the next. But the year 1945 represented a real break in my life. For my personal relations with law and order underwent a profound change after the Liberation and especially after the allied troops entered Germany, accompanied every day by monstrous revelations about the reality of the camps and all the other dark horrors which was the hidden face of National Socialism. (For me the existence of gas chambers is not at issue given that men, women and children died by the millions, innocent of any crime except that of being Jews, gypsies or homosexuals.)

I myself came back from Germany at the end of July 1944 (or the beginning of August, I'm not quite sure), repatriated for reasons of health after a year of STO (*Service du travail volontaire*) and a month in hospital. But during my stay in Nuremberg I hadn't learnt much about the real nature of the Nazi regime.

Fischbach camp was actually a very ordinary labour camp where we were all cooped up together: Serbian peasants conscripted *en masse,* 'voluntary' French workers, young people from Charente and Parisian students who had made the mistake of being born in 1922 (there was a group of about thirty students from the Agro and Grignon who, like everyone else had become semi-skilled workers in a war factory after trying in vain to work in agriculture) as well as other categories and nationalities; but it was an immense camp and we only knew the inmates of three or four neighbouring barracks in the same row as ours who used the same canteen and communal latrines.

Obviously it's hard to stand for seventy-two hours a week at an automatic lathe, especially when—one week in two—you're on night shift; obviously it isn't pleasant or healthy to be fed mainly on rotten potatoes swimming in a greasy sauce; obviously it was cold in winter and the water often froze in our bottles at the foot of our bunks whose mattresses stuffed with straw were swarming with enormous fleas; obviously we had no protection from the regular nightly air raids except the holes in the ground we'd dug ourselves as best we could on Sundays in the frozen snow-covered ground. But many of the Germans were more or less in the same boat, not to mention those who were fighting on the Russian front.

But we weren't ill-treated, nor locked behind concentration camp barbed wire. There were watch towers scattered around but that was because of the risk of fires in the pine forests that spread over most of the countryside. During the far too brief apprenticeship period when we had a little more free time and weren't yet exhausted we could even go to concerts in town or dine in the evening at the village inn and also go for strolls in the country, visiting the small villages nearby (because we had permits as foreign workers, we were allowed to move about within a radius of 100 kilometres around the factory, even if this merely meant getting back to our lodgings which were already three quarters of an hour away by train.) It was the beginning of 1943, it was hot, the people were pleasant, there were very few air raids, the pine trees smelt wonderfully of resin and were protected by notices 'Here only pyromaniacs smoke' and we could go right

90

up to the wild doe who watched us with their large, mild eyes, as it will be—they say—in the Kingdom of Heaven.

But even afterwards when winter came and our working conditions deteriorated, the imagery of order reigning over dear old Germany remained intact. Little blond children still smiled by the roadside; the city pavements were still as neat and nature, whether green or white, still clean; the impeccable soldiers of the Wehrmacht still marched with their heavy tread singing in unison in their deep voices; trains arrived on time; the overseers carried on their drudgery; but if we had to wait in the smoke filled waiting-room in the main station for a convoy that had been delayed by sabotage on the line that was quickly repaired, the officers on leave (they too had tired faces under their flat, rigid helmets) would share their apples with the French students telling them how much they loved Paris, Notre Dame and *Pelléas*.

In fact the only disruption was caused by the English or American air force which, with no visible effect on the war effort (the incendiary bombs seemed to prefer our modest barracks to the imposing M.A.N. factory) methodically destroyed the spruce medieval city and considerably disturbed what sleep was left to us in our new convict life, making it all the more exhausting. And when, at the end of my tether, I lay paralysed on my mattress with acute rheumatoid arthritis I was taken to an underground hospital in a region that had been spared (Ansbach) where doctors and nurses looked after me normally, often kindly.

There was a huge placard in front of Nuremberg station painted in lurid colours depicting scenes of crime, madness (fires, rapes, murders, massacres, etc.) an apocalyptic vision with this caption in Gothic type: 'Victory, or else Bolshevic chaos!' It is not chaos that reigns in the USSR, quite the contrary. Under the Soviet regime too it is absolute order that breeds horror.

And suddenly everything falls apart. The upright generous soldiers, the neat pretty little nurses, the apples of friendship, the tame doe and the fair children's smiles—it was all a hoax. Or rather, only represented half the system, the half visible from the outside, the shop window as it were; and now we were amazed to discover the back of the shop where demented soldiers cut the throats of children, nurses and doe in silence (voiceless screams and silent laughter—the stuff of nightmares.)

Then we remember a few signs that had occasionally shocked us, fugitive crackling in the smooth polished surface of the shop window, quickly covered up by a reassuring 'There's a war on, you know!' that actually explained nothing...In a baker's in Nuremberg, a notice just like other notices (such as 'Closed on Mondays' or 'Please do not handle the bread') calmly announced 'No cakes sold to Jews or Poles'. Human beings, in fact, were divided into distinct categories which didn't have the same rights.

We ourselves didn't wear any badges or distinguishing marks on our clothes (the administration merely deducted in advance a considerable part of our wages under the headings: 'surtax for foreign workers' that is, for those who come and live here at our expense ...) but the German Jews, as in France, wore a yellow star on their chests (besides there were very few around in 1944, we know why), the Ukranians were distinguished by the word *Ost* in white on a blue square (an abbreviation of *Ostarbeiter,* worker from the East), and the Poles, the dear Poles whom the French, for once unanimous, always take to their hearts, could be recognised by the letter 'P' sewn on their clothes and so had no right to strudel or to the triangles of coloured pastry topped with ersatz cream...When one loves order one classifies. And when one has classified one sticks labels on. What could be more natural?

And then an image from the hospital in Ansbach...I'm no longer in the tiny underground room crowded together with the dying and helpless who are too ill to go down to the shelters when there's an air raid warning; it was silent as a morgue and every morning a modest curtain was drawn round those who had died in the night (there was a rail around each bed for this purpose, two metres from the ground). In the long, bright room with two rows of fifty iron bedsteads, one on the window side and the other against the blind wall, right opposite me there's a surprisingly tall, big man with the face of a peaceful beast who seems as strong as an ox; but he's probably in the last stages of tuberculosis judging by his interminable cough and horrible bouts of spitting.

One day they come for him: four soldiers who obviously aren't nurses or doctors. The man refuses to move and begins to bellow loudly in his cavernous, bass voice, interspersed with words in Russian or a similar language. The nice nurses turn away looking embarrassed; they explain to us that this patient is incurable and must be transferred to another hospital. Now on his feet he is struggling feebly still bawling like a beast about to be lead to the slaughter; he apparently knows very well what kind of hospital they mean. Those in charge dress him and end up dragging him away as best as they can. They don't even come up to his shoulder. He seems to belong to a different species from his guards. The badge *Ost* is sewn onto his coat...When one wants to order everything in a man's life one must also take care to order his death.

When I was still being given aspirins in the Fischbach camp infirmary some Charentais peasants had trapped a doe in the snow. Too easy. And certainly not a very clever thing to do. The foresters looked after the herd lovingly in winter, counting them and bringing them bales of straw and hay. The tracks in the virgin snow—of victim and poacher—made the inquest a foregone conclusion, particularly since—like any proud hunter—this one had kept a foot as a trophy. I don't know what became of him, any way I never saw him again in Fischbach.

But our Parisian male nurse, a serious, dedicated medical student, accused of sheltering patients who were faking illness (since they were well enough to hunt in the nearby forest) and in addition accused of hiding their criminal activities (since he hadn't denounced the culprit) was also taken away. He re-appeared a few months later just before I went back to France. He was so changed that I had trouble recognising him. Emaciated, with hands that trembled slightly, his eyes sunk into their enlarged sockets seemed constantly filled with horror; he now only spoke rarely and hesitantly and instantly fell silent when it was a question of what had happened to him during the interval. He was like the English officer in a Kipling story who comes back from Srinagar after being held captive by the Russians...To his friends who pressed him with questions the former nurse ended

93

by conceding this one sentence: 'I have known another kind of camp.'

And even that was, after all, a camp from which you could return. So, during the year 1945 we learned that others existed where the administration had arranged for admission with no return. But between the Fischbach camp and those in the Night and the Fog there could doubtless be found all the intermediary ones, methodically classified and indexed. A very minor detail struck me instantly, perhaps out of all proportion: they were all composed of the same barracks with the same beds...Still more disquieting: the one where I myself lived had previously been used to house the members of congress who'd paraded in the grandiose celebrations of the regime, at the time of the *Reichsparteitage* whose oppressive, pompous buildings (in the typical Hitlerian/Stalinist style) were still standing a few kilometres away.

Although the family unit was as united as ever, except for the fact that my sister, having just graduated from Grignon was working at the time as chief stock breeder on a large farm in Seine-et-Marne, all the members of the clan certainly didn't react in the same way to the shock caused by the German defeat and the dramatic change of perspective on state systems appealing to order. For my mother and father the situation was as clear cut as before and there was no need to modify political options. My mother quite simply refused to believe. As for my father, he calmly declared that if Germany had won it could have uncovered all the war crimes it hoped to find perpetuated by its conquered enemies. International law is the law of the survival of the fittest. The loser is in the wrong. The fact that Soviet Russia, already suspected of being far from guiltless, was simpering on the side of virtue could obviously justify such clichés. And naturally a few questions had to be asked about how useful those two bombs dropped at the last minute on Nagasaki and Hiroshima were to humanity.

At the time of the Liberation my father was disgusted by the French Forces of the Interior's grotesque, last minute hullabaloo and by the pusillanimity of the good people who suddenly turned Gaullist and martial with the same enthusiasm that they had, a short time ago, applauded Pétain and the armistice—like those girls, proletarian or bourgeois, who instantly offered their beds, their sheets still damp, to the new contingent of victorious soldiers. There was also the gaucherie of the gum chewing American G.I's which—at least in my father's eyes—formed a dramatic and unfortunate contrast to the military correctness of our occupying troops, even when on the run.

I'm sure that all this made him feel as if he himself had just lost the war for the second time. Everything he detested was about to begin all over again, worse than ever: licence, demagogy, individual profit, the parliamentary sham, the 'whipped dog politics' (lying back and drifting with the current) and the collapse of the French. He didn't, however, launch into insults or lamentation, but I do remember this simple prophecy: 'This time, children, we'll be lucky if we hang on to Corsica!'

He didn't harbour the same kind of resentment against the Americans as he did against the English; he even felt a vague sympathy for this distant people, which perhaps dated from Lafayette and the shared victory against the English enemy. But the way the American air force had carelessly bombed our Breton and Norman towns and villages (the small city of Aunay-sur-Odon, five kilometres away, was rased to the ground 'by mistake' the day after the Germans left, while the whole population was celebrating its new liberty) left him feeling that the Reich army had above all been conquered by a huge industrial machine; he forgot that four years before the *Panzer-Divisionen* and the *Luftwaffe* had played a somewhat similar role. Paradoxically, the German tanks were to the credit of the courageous recovery of an industrious nation, whereas the tanks and bombers of the United States only proved the detestable power of money.

I was twenty-three years old, but today I have the curious feeling that it was only then that I began to grow up. Bretons are not famed for being precocious. There were no showdowns or clashes at home where I was again living after my Bavarian interlude.

95

Meanwhile, without always consciously realising it, I saw things differently from then on. While fully understanding my father and mother's reactions it was now impossible for me to agree with them on certain crucial points.

In particular, a respect for order at all costs could now only make me profoundly suspicious, to say the least. We'd just seen where that got us. If you had to accept the other side of the coin too, the price was definitely too high. Since I don't believe that Hitler or Stalin were accidents of history: even if they were clinically insane they did actually represent the logical conclusion of the systems they incarnated. And if we really have to choose between that and disorder there's no doubt I would choose disorder.

However, I'm not saying that, traumatised as I was, I instantly relinquished the ideological need for order and classification. This need is very much alive in all of us, side by side with the desire for freedom—its opposite—and everyone has that too. These two opposing forces within us are in constant interaction, both in our conscious mind and in the depths of our unconscious. It's simply a matter of proportion and human beings differ according to the particular form this tortuous duality takes within each individual. My father himself seems to have been a typical example of this insoluble inner contradiction: sensitive individualist yet pro-fascist if need be, an anarchist in his soul yet staunch supporter of an absolute monarchy by divine right (tempered however by regicide), loyal Pétainist, happy to replace the republic's 'Liberty. Fraternity. Equality' by the slogan of the new order: 'Work. Family. Nation' and yet instinctively hostile to any herd mentality whatsoever.

And so within me the proportions were changing: the two irreconcilable forces no longer worked in the same way as before and the new tension which resulted couldn't be expressed in such simple positions any more. There was no question of replacing the Statistics Institute by terrorist action, nor even by leftist agit prop; but I was quite naturally drawn to problematic experimentation in fiction and its contradictions (I have to stress once more that this is how I see my adventure today) as the most promising arena in which to act out this permanent imbalance: the fight

96

to the death between order and freedom, the insoluble conflict between rational classification and subversion, otherwise called disorder.

In the Fifties and Sixties right-minded leftists strongly reproached me because my writing was 'non-committed' and even blamed me for its 'demobilising influence on the young.' Firstly, I was coming from somewhere else and didn't necessarily feel I was in the best position to preach in the market place to my fellow citizens on institutions and their possible changes (revolutionary or reformist); I had no inclination to imitate my numerous ex-Stalinist colleagues who, in the name of their own mistakes (confessions which for the most part lacked sincerity), have not ceased to indoctrinate us. But there's more to it. Just as you can hardly stay in the French Communist Party for twenty long years (long, since they are sown with ever recurring difficulties and strewn with bitter pills) without being steadfastly militant, maintaining a partisan attitude that will swallow anything, so I think I see in myself a very ancient refusal of all militant faith *a fortiori,* a refusal of commitment as Sartre defined it.

During the period of my adolescent submission to codes of moral order and the political right I'm afraid I already always felt more or less of an amateur, a dilettante. Even my nationalism at that time—the most admissible of traditional right wing attributes—seems to have been somewhat suspect. My mother experienced things much more intensely, discussed everything passionately and I remember her reproaching me at the beginning of the war for appearing unconcerned about the Germans' lightning advance into Poland. I'd justified myself, but in a sense she was right. For in June 1940 I certainly was affected by the dramatic rout of our troops, nevertheless I was still behind a pane of glass, as it were.

We had been living in Kerangoff since general mobilisation and hadn't gone back to Paris for the beginning of the Autumn term because there were no more maths classes at the Lycée Buffon (nor anywhere else in Paris). Fortunately my mother was well again since she'd been 'radio-ed' (according to father—a

97

word that we all immediately adopted: the idiolect of small exclusive clans is of necessity composed of words they've made up or twisted). And although she still spent part of the night reading the papers which my father sent on from Paris, the rest of the time she was very busy running the house and feeding the whole household which included, as well as grandmother, godmother (who did the shopping), my sister and I, our two first cousin refugees from the lycée in Brest like us, and also a friend of the same age who was boarding with us.

(After the war our mother's often dormant energies found a new outlet and she flourished once more at Kerangoff: single-handed she designed and supervised the complete reconstruction of the large family house that had been almost totally demolished by allied bombing, 'a hundred percent disaster, according to local experts. My mother would say that she was much happier with large undertakings than with petty daily tasks.)

No, I wasn't indifferent, that's not at all what I remember. But, doubtless, deep down it wasn't me who was losing the battle. For ages I'd thought of our governments as puppet governments, our present-day generals as inept and our army as having been demolished by the Popular Front. I did, therefore, have trouble suddenly identifying with a France that had been so utterly discredited. I was simply condemned to accept what others had been preparing for me for a long time now. Of course I can't claim to have attempted any move in the other direction; but at seventeen what could I have done? The stupidly reassuring news broadcast by the authorities added still further to the feeling of impotence and abandon. We were fed lies like children.

Maybe also my firm conviction that I belonged to a very small clan, absolutely separate from the masses, a belief carried to extremes by the clan's ideology (we, the Robbe-Grillet's were accused of considering the rest of the world as a bunch of imbeciles)was hardly conducive to the sudden national solidarity demanded of me. Finally there was our distance from the battle-fields. This end of Finistére was miles and miles away from the Vistula. The Rhine, Meuse or Somme were scarcely much closer. I lived in another world. I worked hard at school ('top of the class' according to my school report—but I've always loved learning and still do); I did my homework at home conscientiously, I did well in exams ...I was a demilitarised zone, a solitary unofficial observer, forgotten in an open city ...

The war broke in on us suddenly, in an unexpected form: my father was left at the garden gate in mid-afternoon by a military driver in a battered car whose bodywork, crudely repainted in drab grey to avoid being spotted by the enemy aircraft was, nevertheless, pitted in several places with the marks of the Stukas machine guns. My father was pale and his usual nervous state was much more pronounced than usual. He told us what had happened in short, dry, neutral sentences, as briefly as possible.

Having burned the useless records of our armaments in the courtyard of the ministery he had set out in a convoy going south, soon lost in the flood of the exodus—neither civilians nor soldiers knew what they were advancing towards. The bridges over the Loire had been destroyed and they had to find another further to the west. Feeling that he was of no use in the midst of this débâcle where he merely added to the confusion, he had then decided to get back to Brest, to the only beings he felt responsible for; this had been relatively easier since those roads were less crowded with fugitives. Desertion of his post? But he no longer had a post! Anyway, our father had once declared that he was capable of anything, even murder, to protect his own family.

That day he also said that the war was lost, irretrievably, that we had no material, no army, no allies, no resources of any kind ...At times he could hardly bring out the words—because of anguish or the suppressed tears of defeat, or because he was so moved at actually finding us all again. My mother kept repeating: 'Are you sure?' She didn't want to believe it was all over, that now there was no protest possible, no miracle to hope for ...She wept with indignation. The driver went off in his battered car to try to find his own family through the German lines. It's not surprising that Marshal Pétain appeared like a guiding light in the midst of such a disaster.

And so we had the occupation: omnipresent but with no com-

99

motion; it functioned smoothly and was fairly unobtrusive from the outside except for a few parades with music blaring which were viewed as slightly comical if anything. The German soldiers were polite, young, smiling; they gave the impression of being serious, full of good will, almost engaging as if they wanted to apologise for having entered our peaceful territory uninvited. They radiated discipline and neatness. (The very exceptional rapists and looters had instantly been harshly punished by their superiors). Whether they were dressed in green or black, people at first contemplated these tall, blond boys who drank water and sang in unison as if they were some strange animal. On a large propaganda poster (that had replaced Paul Reynaud's 'We will conquer because we are the strongest') one of them was helping a little girl across the street, holding her hand; the caption read 'Trust the German soldier'. Certainly in 1940-41 the picture and text didn't seem shockingly provocative. If you haven't lived through that time it's difficult to see that Vercors' famous novel, printed by the Editions de Minuit clandestinely, was a book of the Resistance. People kept saying 'At least they're decent!' France deep-down heaved a sigh of relief.

And doubtless when all's said and done, being on the sidelines suited me quite well too. We weren't on one side or the other any more, we had got rid of the English yet had no real commitment to the German side. Thanks to the Marshal we had suddenly, miraculously become a neutral country like Switzerland ... Better still: disarmed! Our eventual allegiance to one camp or the other was sort of put in brackets; even our most impassioned views were now merely a subject for friendly discussion, with the family, in the neighbourhood café or in bitchy exchanges with cantankerous neighbours.

I could calmly go on being a disinterested amateur, a witness on unpaid leave. The occupation was a bit like the 'phoney war': terrible things were going on all over the world that were likely to be of vital importance for our future, but for the time being we were excluded. We only heard about them from a distance, through papers which mostly had to be read between the lines and from the radio which didn't even disguise its partisan and propagandist nature. Pétain's 'wait and see policy' (real collaborators blamed him enough for it) looked like political wisdom and national vocation at one and the same time.

What else could be done? Carry on the fight courageously underground or by crossing the Channel to help England deliver us one day? Join the bitter European crusade against the communist hydra? I knew a very few boys who threw themselves into the fray in one or other of these causes. They were seen as kids looking for a good scrap rather than heroes. As one of Beckett's characters would say: 'Let's do nothing, it's safer!'

The family had returned to Paris. I studied for two years for the Agro exams at the Lycée St. Louis in the same class as my sister and got into the Agro with a very good grade in the autumn of 1942. As Brest was out of bounds from then on, we spent our summers at Guingamp with our Aunt, Mathilde Canu who taught arithmetic in a school in the town. All around was woodland, the old Breton earth growing oaks and ferns. One memory among others: the small street where we lived led to the cemetery; a detachment of verdigris soldiers passes under our window and disappears in that direction; the first six are carrying a coffin on their shoulders, the others follow, their leaden steps accentuated by their heavy boots on the uneven, glistening paving stones. These are no longer the fine young men of the invasion but reservists, doubtless ill-equipped to endure the hardships of the Eastern Front. They're singing in unison: 'I had a comrade...' in slow, bass voices, utterly despairing. A fine drizzle is falling on the meagre column making its way down the middle of the street and over the whole town adding its Celtic note to the nostalgia of the old song from beyond the Rhine in memory of dead companions.

The capital wasn't very jolly either; it too was emptied of cars and silent, which gave it a new beauty. And the German troops hadn't crowded it out with patrols or tourists: obviously they had better things to do. The Parisian pedestrian enjoyed a sort of freedom in this vacuum: the freedom of desert spaces, or abandonment or sleep. We went for long aimless strolls through the phantom city. Once my father and I pushed a rented barrow from one end of the city to the other to bring back a providential sack of coal. At home in winter the cold was a problem, plus the constant scarcity of food; worry about prosaic essentials often took precedence over all the rest. My father devoted himself body and soul to the material support of the clan.

Once I had got into the Agro and was at last certain of completing my long, costly studies I worked a little less enthusiastically, or rather, I chose the subjects I was interested in (such as plant biology, genetics, biochemistry, geology...) neglecting the others (agricultural mechanisation, rural engineering or industrial technology). I went to a lot of concerts and to the opera. There were certainly numerous German officers there and they were even in the majority in the stalls in some famous concert halls, particularly at the Palais Garnier. But they didn't worry me: they were a very quiet audience, almost shadowy in their stiff uniforms; and didn't we all appreciate the same music: Bach, Beethoven, Wagner, Debussy, Ravel? Anyway, their seats were much too dear for my meagre pocket money: paradoxically I was the one looking down on them from on high.

There were 'societies' at the Institut agronomique, small groups of students with the same interests: bridge, chess, riding, dancing. With a few friends, including the future painter Bernard Dufour, we'd started the 'Agro music society'; but as most of its memebers were openly Pétainist, our class mates, who pretended to consider us as shocking collaborators, called us—quite amicably—the 'K group'. Since the entry of the United States into the war and the German difficulties on the Eastern front, the Gaullists had increased in number. But all this was in the realm of speculation and didn't cause any animosity or real divisions between the opposed factions.

One day, however, in a mischievous mood (I always enjoyed provoking my fellow students) I had pinched a bundle of papers that two 'anglophile' students were perusing with a mysterious air at the top of the lecture hall. Amazement: they contained detailed plans for the defence of Paris! On seeing their sudden anxiety I realised that they were playing at being Resistance fighters more actively—if not more effectually—than I'd thought. I was even more surprised when I realised they were afraid that I'd denounce them. I immediately gave the compromising papers back. This quite natural gesture, as I thought, earned me the benefit of a similar indulgence in the autumn of 1944 when in the middle of the hysterical purges in the second and last year of our course I was back again with my maquisard classmates, or simply the shirkers.

At the end of spring 1943 all students born in 1922 were called up for the *STO, Service du travail obligatoire*. This was supposedly instead of the military service from which the 'class of 1922' had been exempted; but this time there was no possibility of deferment even for those who had just a few more months left before graduating. The civilian mobilisation was under the pretext of 'relieving' our soldiers: we were going to work in Germany to replace prisoners of war who, thanks to us, could then return home after three years in captivity.

Did we believe this? We half believed it. Anyway, we were suckers. But the old Marshal needed us. In the papers you saw edifying photos of families with tears of happiness in their eyes, greeting a father or a husband who had returned after such a long absence. We were also promised work in agriculture, from which a large number of the liberated prisoners would be returning. We could, therefore, think of this compulsory stay as a sort of practical training, like the stint we'd done the year before in civic rural service and on French farms, between our exams and the beginning of the course. The director of the Institute came to the main lecture hall to address the two classes assembled in this emergency and to urge us to go. I remember his peroration: 'Go to Germany, young people, you will get to know a great country.' At the time of the Liberation he'd been a long standing member of the Resistance and therefore, had no trouble keeping his job. And, without the least embarassment he welcomed us back to the college with an appropriate speech.

Of course the K group were easily persuaded to go. But so were many others too. The ones who got out of it were mainly those who took advantage of close peasant connections and hoped to find conditions more favourable to a semi-clandestine existence in the provinces. In exchange for our obedience to the call, we the enlisted men, would be provided with a train ticket to

103

Bavaria, a new pair of galoshes, a tin of sardines in oil and a ticket to go and hear Edith Piaf in some huge Parisian theatre ... We were setting off to relieve the prisoners, Piaf was singing for us, Pétain smiled under his white moustache ...I put on the galoshes, gave the sardines to my mother and listened liked a good boy, to Edith Piaf, a minute, touching figure in the far distance facing rows and rows of seats filled with the departing labour conscripts.

After this, along with other students from the Agro and Grignon I was back in Nuremberg, city of Hans Sachs and the Mastersingers, a lathe operator in a heavy armaments factory specialising in the manufacture of the famous Panther tanks. But our two month apprenticeship was almost like a holiday. As work didn't begin for the novices till midday, we had our mornings free to wander in the pine forests and meadows near the camp. Thanks to provisions that our families had managed to send, we played at cooking our lunch on small stoves that we knocked up outside the barracks. At the factory the theory classes consisted of inculcating the rudiments of mathematics, which was obviously more important for our Yugoslav comrades whose knowledge of the subject wasn't so extensive as that of the students from the top colleges. Anyhow, our instructor who was Turkish (and whose so-called linguistic prowess must have originated in the bizarre mixture that made up our class) spoke to us in a strange language—directly modelled on German grammatical structures with in addition a vocabulary consisting of a large number of more or less gallicised words—so that we weren't always able to tell when he switched from French to Serbo-Croat. Luckily some of the same phrases came up everyday and we ended up understanding them.

Here for example is the ritual opening of anything to do with using an automatic lathe: 'The first, normal, what do you do? So, gentlemen, receive you face-plate material...' i.e. you begin by fixing the part into the mandrel. The mandrel is called *Patten-Futter* in German; as for the verb 'receive', *bekommen*, which is an all-purpose word in colloquial speech, rather like 'to check' in American, our teacher made liberal use of it, as he had an extremely limited vocabulary.

But fairly soon, having had enough of our sniggering incomprehension he preferred to address himself to the Serbian half of his audience. The key phrase informing us that the 'French' class had just ended was 'So, gentlemen, get on with you private work' which meant we were then free to write to our families undisturbed. (My long detailed letters must also be in the low beamed attic in Kerangoff— favourite territory for us children when it rained—with the tender, illegible daily reports my father wrote to my mother during their temporary separations, seasonal or accidental, and also the even older, rarer letters—the mail ships weren't very frequent at the end of the last century—sent by Grandfather Canu from China, Tonkin or Valparaiso).

Immediately after, the signal *'Akotomaserbé'* woke up the other side of the room; but we could tell that this was still a mispronounciation of our language: 'Listen to me, Serbs!' Never being sure of understanding what's going on, constantly interpreting, accepting guesswork, uncertainty, ambiguity, gaps in communication as your normal relation with the world was now part of our life and also, in a sense, constituted its exotic attraction. After all, this was my first holiday abroad, since in the past the Vaudois frontier hadn't been particularly disorienting as regards language.

During practicals with the metal working tools or on the machines, the foreman was so benevolent and disenchanted that with a smile of impotence he agreed to clock in for Dufour and I at the right time when we wanted to leave the factory early in order not to miss the beginning of a concert. *'Franzoz, grosse Lump!'* he concluded philosophically; this gave me the chance to hear in particular all of Beethoven's sonatas for cello and piano at the Katherinenkirche—ravishing setting for chamber music in a small white and gold baroque church.

I really had the feeling—a mixture of flippancy, distance and suspense—that I was merely a tourist. Handling files, the vice, lathe or drilling machine seemed just like a game to me, as I love manual labour, and I even began to make a steel chess set (for my own amusement) which I didn't finish, alas, like so many other things. But a few weeks later, even when I was part of the production line and obeying the forced rhythms that left no time for rest or day dreaming, standing every day in front of my grinding machine for two shifts of five-and-a-half hours at a stretch, polishing within five hundredth of a millimetre—with no scope for deviation or imagination—the monstrous crankshafts of the tanks (which were so heavy they had to be lifted by an electric hoist) my life had certainly changed abruptly and completely but I still felt convinced I was only a tourist.

The life of a semi-skilled worker is a hopeless one and yet at no time did I despair: I was only passing through and had no real past or future link with this factory—aimless, I was there by chance, by mistake as it were. And on Saturday evenings when a small poster with its swastika appeared above the clocking in machines, informing us that we had to work on Sundays ...for the German Fatherland, the war effort, final victory etc., I managed, after a fashion, to translate the text, up to the words in bold type: 'Your Führer needs you!'and didn't feel in the least involved. Of course I'd have to work all the next day like my comrades on the production line, Bavarians, Swabians, Franconians, but unlike them—and I could see the difference in their drawn faces—I didn't feel in any way committed to the business because I should never have been doing this work: I wasn't a real worker, I wasn't German, he wasn't my Führer and in any case this eventual victory wouldn't be mine either.

I could see quite a few comrades around me who certainly seemed to be better equipped to identify with the improvised role they were made to play; sometimes even professed Gaullists, working for the enemy war effort with a conviction I totally lacked, and this made it easier for me to gauge the fundamental *strangeness* of my own relation with the world, which was doubtless more serious than the simple fact of expatriation. Whereas, with no thought of sabotage, without the slightest ill will, I never managed to machine finish correctly the number of parts specified (I am good with my hands but not with machines), the others in a few days had become real grinding or milling machine operators, or whatever else.

Once when I was in the infirmary revelling in one of the early works of Ilya Ehrenburg, *Les aventures de Julio Jurenita* (the stock of discarded books that made up the camp's French library seemed to come primarily from the Nazi auto-da-fé) I offered to show a young French peasant due to be sent back to work because he was better, how to fix the thermometer by gently rubbing the mercury bulb with a woollen sock. But the boy answered that he preferred to get back to his machine because of 'the wife and kids who were starving to death in La Roche, Indre-sur-Loire;' a doubly absurd pretext since the social security system which was quite good for its time would have paid him the same wages if he were ill and because, on the other hand, as I heard later, he didn't have a wife or children. He was hoping for the Allied landing but he already clung to his position as a German worker. He missed his drilling machine.

On the contrary, the feeling of exteriority, almost of extra-territoriality, that I experienced so strongly (remaining on the outside, being there by accident, as the result of an amusing rather than tragic misunderstanding) stayed with me even at night when the air raid warnings went off, immediately followed by the dull roar of the bombers, tearing us out of our precious sleep as we had to leap from our bunks and leave the barracks some of which would soon go up in flames. The sky was lit up by clusters of incandescent flares drifting slowly down towards us (to light up the targets?) diffusing a bright pink glow punctuated by short white bursts from the anti-aircraft guns, while the pine forests in flames ('Here only pyromaniacs smoke!') were already dyeing large patches of the horizon a smokey orange.

Doubtless the fact that we weren't in the town heightened the theatrical quality of the scene. The camp was strewn with incendiary bombs that went off on the ground like dud fireworks. And even when we threw ourselves flat on the grass as we heard the big bombs whining and waited for the muffled crash of the final explosion, imagining it to be right beside us with the earth trembling so violently, once again, despite the danger, it was as if the fact that I was there by mistake played a decisive part in my safety: I was not at war with these planes, their bombs weren't aimed at me, even if I were to be killed I would still be the odd man out in the casualty lists—one superfluous corpse as if I were a phantom metal worker, accidentally accounted

107

for in the production statistics.

Maybe it was only in the morning, back in the damaged city, that I felt more as if I'd lost something, a part of myself had gone forever, or at least I felt a pained sympathy—although useless, impotent and, therefore, of no practical help—in front of the shapeless ruins of a pretty baroque church which had been lovingly looked after for centuries, or facing the charred remains of the big wooden houses with their flower balconies dating from the Middle Ages, beside the clear waters of the Pegnitz. Every night a little piece of old Europe was disappearing in dust and smoke ...But isn't nostalgia for ruins—even recent ones—one of the traditional ingredients of the journey into the unknown?

And it's still that sensation of being an isolated, protected visitor behind a pane of glass that I experience once again a few years later at the camp at Divotino in the green hills of Bulgaria surrounded by fields of maize and tall sunflowers; I'm with Daniel Boulanger (whom I'd met in Prague a month before at the time of the vast phoney congress for so-called 'democratic youth') and Claude Ollier (whom I knew in Nuremberg in the Summer of 1943); we are all three volunteers in the 'International Reconstruction Brigade'; this time I'm wielding a pick axe and shovel on the future track of the Pernik-Voloviek railway line. After I came back, in a text published about 1950 in an engineering magazine and reprinted in 1978 in the review *Obliques,* I wrote about the utter absurdity of the work done on this site, the air of impenetrable mystery surrounding the recruitment of the young Bulgarian members of the 'brigade', the rambling Marxist-Leninist propaganda speeches (for peace, of course and friendship between nations), punctuated by our chanting in unison, harking on the names of the heroes: 'Stalin! Thorez! Tito! Dimitrov! until we burst into uncontrollable laughter; and I wrote about the ever widening gulf in the French delegation between the real militant Communists and the others. Whether on the right or the left my attempts at commitment certainly didn't agree with me.

In the same issue of *Obliques* François Jost collected evidence

—photos, press cuttings, quotations from books, etc.—of another biographical episode where, once more, I am distinctly (abnormally?) distanced from something—extremely dramatic—that's happening to me: a plane crash. I was with my wife on the first Air France Boeing 707 on the Paris-Tokyo flight that crashed on take off after the Hamburg stopover. This was in the early days of the polar flights in the summer of 1961.

At the Atlantic hotel, where the uninjured passengers who wished to continue their journey by the next long-haul flight were staying, I was questioned on the phone by a journalist from the *A.F.P.* and reported what I had just witnessed as accurately as I could, as I had been sitting at a window right in the tail of the plane which gave me a clear view: the plane does not taxi down the centre of the runway, the grass verge on the left comes, closer and closer while we keep on going, the wing dips suddenly on that side, one of the engines hits the ground and catches fire, the plane tilts in the opposite direction tearing off the undercarriage and a second engine but still keeps moving on its belly over a terrain that's by no means flat, etc.

The remains of the fuselage, cut into three sections, came to a halt in a 'Z' shape. Flames at least twenty metres high burst from the fuel tanks. Both sitting in the tail of the plane Catherine and I found ourselves without a scratch, half-buried in a fragment of the cabin. Stupidly, I stop to look for her handbag—although there's nothing of value in it—among the seats, most of which have been torn loose, while the air hostesses are yelling outside 'Run! It's going to explode!' But the Japanese in their socks hurrying across the bumpy ground through fragments and debris nevertheless turn round several times towards the brazier to take the photographs that will constitute the indisputable high spot of their trip to Europe.

Soon after, while the ambulance men are still freeing those who were seriously injured (no one was killed as the plane was almost empty and all the seats at the points where the plane broke up were, by chance, empty), when the firemen are still not sure that they've put out all the fires (the plane didn't explode in the end) and as thick black smoke was still gushing out, swirling above the thickly spread dry ice, a small Air France van pulls up right alongside the plane, a painter in a white overall gets out, very professional, leans his extension ladder against the shattered fuselage, climbs up with his materials and calmly begins to paint out the too famous Air France sea-horse. An expert plane spotter could probably recognise the shattered Boeing, but all 707's look alike, and none of the passenger who are again taking off on the runway, staring goggle-eyed at the disturbing remains, need know to whom this one belonged.

Painter, firemen, ambulances ...Yet another car has arrived on the scene, one of the first to make its way across the ground that's not suitable for vehicles, the so-called rescue vehicle: a grey-green van, inside entirely covered with shelves filled with brandy glasses ...the first-aid barman was himself trembling so violently from shock that he spilled half his cognac ...One more image that recurs insistently: the crazy slope we had to climb up, having got through the wide open door, to get out of the hole we were buried in, where Catherine's high heeled shoes were left behind...

My reporter on the other end of the line doubtless considers that I am singularly lacking in a flare for the sensational: my account quite rightly seems to him to be fairly objective but somewhat dull, whereas he has to make the accident as dramatic as possible. So, he has no hesitation in putting words into my mouth for tomorrow's press release broadcast by all the *France-Presse* correspondents: a totally different version crammed with grandiloquent metaphors and stereotyped emotion. I read this two days later in Japan and am if anything, amused. But then a week afterwards my story, taking up a whole page spread in *L'Express,* has turned into a so-called literary scandal. Despite the article's trumped up tone the author obviously really thinks that this time I've been unmasked: my alleged account (which he pretends to believe is authentic, although he himself has been a reporter for many years on a magazine with a vast circulation and, therefore, knows the unscrupulous practices of the profession) proves that my writing as a novelist is merely contrived, fraudulent, since when frightened I suddenly start talking like everyone else and 'tell the story of the crash purely and simply'!

And here's what 'purely and simply' is: 'In an infernal uproar the plane left the runway and began churning up the field, furrowing like a plough', etc. Even amongst the staff of L'Express I can't see who would speak like this in everyday life albeit after surviving an air crash. But the most amusing repercussion was the appearance of L'oeuvre ouverte in the bookshops several months later; it's a fascinating essay on modern literature in which Umberto Eco, using extremely cogent arguments (the language of the writer, he says, is different from the language he uses for daily communication), defends me in particular against the sarcastic pamphleteer—thus giving credence to my authorship of the ravings published by the A.F.P. as well as to the violent agitation which must have provoked them.

I am here dwelling on the successive stages of this adventure firstly, in order to point out once more that what we have inherited from the worst of Zola is, in the eyes of the general public and its official spokesmen, supposedly the most natural way of speaking and writing. But also in order to examine my actual reactions at the time of this abortive take off. On the one hand I'm sure that I was alert enough behind my window pane, to follow second by second the different stages of the accident. On the other hand, I maintain that everything happened far too fast for there to be time to be afraid. But Catherine, who was sitting two or three rows further forward and wasn't right next to a window—preferring a book to the view—says, on the contrary, that such a series of shocks lasts an interminable length of time and that the fear she experienced during those long moments haunted her afterwards for many years to come.

In fact, having agreed—probably after taking tranquillisers administered officially—to set off again the next day for Tokyo by air (on that occasion we didn't have the time to take the Transiberian Express because we had to be back for the Venice film festival where Marienbad's fate was to be decided—this was the film's last chance) then, having returned with me to Rome by easy stages via Hong Kong (shaken up by an ill-timed typhoon over the China sea), Bangkok, Delhi and Teheran (where all her paternal family lived), getting more and more frightened at each successive flight, even when the plane was as smooth as the smoothest of Paris metros—like Zeno's arrow—she even managed to communicate her anxiety to me by osmosis and had to give up travelling by air for ten years; this gave us the opportunity to range over the Old and the New Worlds by rail as well as crossing the oceans of the North and South on luxurious liners that are now extinct.

When we were on one of our last New York-Cherbourg crossings aboard the commercial but already mythical *Queen Elizabeth II* there was an incident that reproduced, yet again, the same thought provoking elements: danger, instant spectacle, journalists' evident disappointment in the face of any account that lacks pathos, hyperbolic distortions of the story dramatised to titillate the masses. We're at sea, Catherine, my sister Anne-Lise and I, on the third day of our crossing, roughly half way between the American and the French coast. We emerge from the cinema, a huge auditorium worthy of the Champs Elysées, where we've just seen (in English, which none of us understands) a film in which an airliner got into serious difficulties in mid-flight; I don't remember the details. It's in the afternoon and we take one of the big lifts that serves eleven or twelve decks and go up to the upper deck to get some air.

The ship is motionless; we don't know why but we do know this is odd. The lifeboats are at emergency stations: hoisted outboard in their davits above the water as if ready to be lowered for an abandon ship exercise. A few dozen sailors are bustling round them. They're all wearing life jackets and sou'westers like Newfoundland fishers in a storm. The sky's overcast, lowering. The ocean's as calm as it can be in the middle of the North Atlantic. People strolling about, vaguely anxious, are discussing possibilities in different languages.

Various rumours run rife and soon an official announcement from the captain informs us that there may be bombs on board, no one knows where, planted by terrorists who are demanding an enormous ransom from Cunard and, if their demands aren't met, threatening to blow up the whole ship; we are waiting for

112

bomb disposal experts from England to defuse the bombs. Immediately all the passengers dash to their cabins only to rush back with cameras and movie equipment which they'd run off to fetch without a moment's delay: what a piece of luck—they'll be able to film the arrival of the military aircraft, the dropping of the frogmen and bomb disposal equipment and maybe even— if their luck holds—the explosion, the shipwreck and their own deaths ...

The beginning of the operation fulfils their expectations: the three planes emerge from the clouds diving several times one after the other in the direction of the liner, doubtless to plot its exact position. Then they drop four men in black wet suits and also a number of containers, all harnessed to orange parachutes. Three of the lifeboats launched with their crews then have no trouble picking them up, although from the promenade deck they're so far away that we can hardly make out the details of the rescue in the heavy seas.

For some eight hours the immense *Q.E.II*—her engines still turned off—is systematically inspected with the most advanced equipment from top to bottom, above, below, inside. In the middle of the night, a new announcement from the captain finally informs us that the search has proved vain, that in any case nothing has been found near the vital organs of the ship and that we can therefore continue on our way; if it does turn out that there are bombs on board, they can only be of a relatively low explosive power and must be hidden in the cabins (which haven't been searched) so that if there is an explosion it won't interfere with the smooth sailing of the ship. It's hard to tell whether this last detail is an example of the British sense of humour. Anyhow, the rest of the crossing was spent celebrating in honour of the 'good fellows' who risked their lives to save us.

At Cherbourg, the first port of call, all the television networks in Europe and America, as well as all the daily and weekly papers and radio stations etc., are there to welcome us. The reporters rush up but are visibly disappointed by our accounts of the drama: no, no one panicked; yes, people took photos; no, we weren't really frightened, we carried on eating and drinking, watching adventure films, playing jack-pot and lotto; yes, we did, all things considered, enjoy ourselves.. But, in front of the deployment of the mass media, filming us on all sides and hounding us with questions, we really do feel that we're not rising to the occasion. Some of our interviewers are almost angry: for two pins they're ready to blame us for not having been blown to pieces and gone down with the ship, singing in unison 'Nearer, my God, to Thee, nearer to Thee...'

Before, in Hamburg, I'd ended up feeling guilty when my journalist, who was getting more and more irritated on the other end of the line, had finally abandoned his pose of feigned compassion and accused me outright of not being sufficiently moved by the crash. I remember one detail in particular: he really had hoped that I had 'lost all my manuscripts' in the disaster. That at least, in the absence of charred body or survivors maddened by the shock, might make an acceptable scoop: imagine the despair throughout the land of France—from château to humble cottage—when they learnt that the only draft of *L'immortelle* and all the preliminary notes for *La maison de rendezvous* had just gone up in flames forever with 100,000 litres of kerosene...

As I was endeavouring to get across to him that a writer doesn't usually travel with those kinds of things that are precious, cumbersome and heavy, especially when he's going to the other side of the world for preliminary talks on a film project, my enraged interlocutor, at his wits end, hurled at me: 'So really you don't give a damn that all your luggage went up in flames!'

In order to calm him down I was then forced to betray a small personal secret, a meagre titbit: unbeknown to Catherine, I had in my luggage a pretty gold necklace which I was going to give her on the anniversary of our meeting on the Orient Express going to Istanbul, exactly ten years ago on the 4th of August, that is, less than a week after the abortive take-off in which we had just nearly died together.

Ten years already. Thirty-three today ...Summer, 1951, I was stuck on page forty of *Les gommes* and had left Brest on impulse after reading an advertisement in *Combat* for a (very cheap) student trip in Turkey. Old Flaubertian mirage—escape to the

Orient, where time has suddenly stopped...Wallas, puzzling over the stupid riddle of the Sphinx, was waiting beside the choppy waters of his canal enclosed by the liftbridge...he's been waiting for days, for centuries...Immemorial ruins bathed in the bright sun of Asia Minor, shadows cast by the minarets in Sinan onto the esplanades with their uneven pavements where a solitary watchman, wrapped in his caftan squats against a pillar circled with bronze, meditating, beaches dreaming under their fig trees beside the still, limpid sea of Marmara, caïques sailing up the Corne d'Or through the lengthening rays of the setting sun, the main street in Péra already lit by the signs for the dancing girls in the soft twilight among the floods of silent men dressed in black, the Galatasaray Lycée where the sugary, nostalgic melodies *alla turca* throbbed, lulling us to sleep in the big white marble dormitories, the numerous little steamers with their gay plumes of black smoke crossing the Bosphorous in the pale morning light with their motionless passengers wearing fez and heavy moustaches, their bundles wrapped in carpets, their sheep and itinerant tea sellers, the melancholy cry of the yoghurt sellers, the smell of grilled fish and the peach melba that Catherine lived on almost exclusively ...

She looked so young at that time that everyone thought she was a child. Thirteen years old, 'Oh Romeo, Juliet's age!' And people took her for my daughter—while she was searching for traces of her real father, a small boy who survived the Armenian massacres—climbing nimbly up the rustic streets of Kadikoy and Uskudar...The necklace lost in the hold of the Boeing commemorated all that.

I had taken weeks to choose it with love before we left, and now it would never be given to the young girl of my dreams, trifling sentimental treasure buried forever between bitter-sweet memories and oblivion. But, in *L'Express* the next week, my guilty secret had become: 'and when a writer of the *nouveau roman* loses all his luggage he doesn't care a damn about his manuscripts that have been burnt to ashes, but only "his wife's jewellery"!'

In the end, against all expectations, our beautiful new suitcases which were also bought for this trip, were returned to us hardly battered, a few hours later, among a pile of miscellaneous objects that had fallen out of more fragile parcels. On the other hand, the cinema co-production that we were on our way to Japan to set up never got past the screen-play stage, since the wealthy Japanese Hollywood-style company who hired me at great expense certainly didn't have the slightest idea of the unorthodox nature of the narrative structures I'd already been constructing for several years. These people had only called on me as the result of a total misunderstanding, fostered for obscure reasons by a French backer, and which went on for a whole six months.

However, a few months later a blockbuster film was made about the spectacular ransom of the Q.E.II. The French version was called *Terreur sur le Brittanic*. The ominous, imposing sound of the '...itanic' alone already gives the clue: the greatest liner in the world keeling over after a fatal collision. The captain was Omar Sharif, whose Anglo-Saxon appearance may obviously seem a somewhat debatable point, and he had an amorous intrigue with a beautiful blonde in first class, married to someone else, naturally. Terrorist threats in mid-ocean, air-sea rescue teams arriving post-haste from England, the company's equivocations, passengers mastering their *angst* (no question of taking photos), tense silences and looks, etc.

But the parachute drop of frogmen and equipment took place in a violent storm, which is much more commercial, so that several sailors were swept away from their accomodation ladders or buffeted in the foam as they hoisted the precious crates aboard big motor launches bobbing on the crest of thirty foot waves. And this time there 'really' were bombs hidden in the sophisticated bowels of the ship. The first even caused serious damage when they exploded, despite the skill and courage of the glorious bomb disposal experts. The final catastrophe was only avoided in the nick of time—after the statutory hundred minutes of film time. Omar Sharif, toughened by his ordeal, did however resolve, as he stiffened his upper lip, to leave the pretty passengers to their husbands henceforth.

Among the real details of our adventure one of the most noteworthy, which did spell potential tragedy at the time, had been omitted by the script writer. The *QE II* was carrying a whole party of wealthy American paraplegics in their wheel chairs ...But this wasn't a film by Buñuel.

I may have solved the problems of emotive expression and the excessive use of metaphor—at least provisionally—in the Sixties, but this certainly wasn't the case when I began writing *Le régicide* fifteen years earlier. With a rueful smile I can even point to several places in this first attempt at a novel (it wasn't published until much later)—whole passages which doubtless my *A.F.P.* interviewer or the reporter from *L'Express* wouldn't have disowned.

The most obvious of the internal conflicts that structure this narrative is precisely the tension between fact and expression, between 'neutral' writing and the systematic recourse to the pompous attractions of metaphor. In this light the central figure in the text—Boris, the unique, very personal narrative consciousness who even expresses himself half the time in the first person—fits into the illustrious family of the previous decade, through Camus' Meursault and Sartre's Roquentin.

Doesn't the hero of *L'étranger* actually struggle desperately against the world's adjectivity? And isn't it this struggle (perhaps lost in advance) that gives the book its historical importance? Anyway, from the opening pages you do sense the humanising metaphors lying in wait for the objective narrative voice, though it is on the look out; for instance the famous 'drowsy' headland that Sartre in a snap judgement blames on the author's carelessness. It's these metaphors that encroach insidiously every time the dispassionate militancy of a well trained phenomenological technique yields, even momentarily, to sensual pleasure. And of course it is these which, in the long scene of the crime, end by breaking down the last bulwarks of this systematically purified, although supposedly natural style; it then seems to be a mask worn by a noble, unhappy soul who was pretending—doubtless for obscure moral reasons—to be nothing but a pure Husserlian consciousness.

As for the philosopher-figure in *La nausée*, he himself admits that it's the aggressive, viscous contingency of the things that make up the external world, the moment you tear away the thin layer of 'utility' (or merely of sense) protecting us and hiding them, that is at once the source of his metaphysical-visceral unease, the object of his passionate fascination and the initial incitement to keep a diary of 'events' (in other words, of his relations with the world) and so produce a narrative. The two scriptural forces involved here in a fight to the death will be, as we recall, on the one hand the courageous but repellent attempt to capture the events in question; on the other hand, the good old conventional attempt to write, in the style of Balzac, the complete, definitive history of the adventurous life of the Marquis de Rollebon (which is at the same time, alas, enigmatic and full of gaps) a healthy reassuring but profoundly dishonest narrative—beside which Sartre/Roquentin also copies out a whole page of *Eugénie Grandet* as an antidote to nausea, in memory of that happy time when it was thought that adjectives were innocent, reality clear and precise and that it could be represented without pitfalls. In any case, the cure doesn't work for long—it's the past historic alone that overflows the diary's text in the wake of Balzac!

Like these two illustrious godparents (Roqentin and Meursault) Boris also has the all pervading feeling of dislocation, of a division between him and the world—both things and people—which prevents him from really being involved in what's around him, what happens to him, and even his own actions; hence his feeling that he has no reason to exist, that he's superfluous, that he's there by accident so that no sanction—except social—can ever condemn or vindicate him. His decision to kill the king, less (or more) than a mere sexual impulse of the Oedipal type, at first suggests an ultimate attempt to leap over the gulf, to cross the invisible yet immovable dividing wall, at last to get rid of the diptheritic constriction that even stops him breathing (I think it'll now be obvious how I'm deliberately putting the expression of such a desire in sexual terms).

But regicide is also, of course, the killing of the inscription: the inscription of (society's) tables of the law, inscription of death on my tomb. The anagram *'ci-gît-Red'* ('here lies Red') which appears shortly after the crime, would accordingly represent the capital crime's auto-effacement, consequently the failure (inscribed in advance) of the project of liberation. And so I'm hardly in a position to cast the last stone, proclaiming the failure of Sartre and Camus, unless that stone is also consciously added to my own tumulus.

And I'd like to use this to return once more to *L'étranger* which almost certainly had a profound influence on my literary début. It's not particularly good form in trendy intellectual circles to acknowledge the influence of Camus' first novel on a whole generation and even beyond. The huge apparatus of symposia and university theses paying tribute to him throughout the world for forty years, plus his emphatic, immediate and lasting public recognition, not to mention the fact that he has been definitively salvaged by all the school text books, today makes this allusion almost anathema.

And yet I'm not the only writer—of my age or younger—to place him amongst the most significant encounters that stand out as milestones in their development. And if I blithely crossed swords with him in the mid-Fifties, (as I also did with Sartre over *La nausée*), this was as much to point out my debt to each of them as to define the direction of my own work by breaking away from them. Besides, every time I reread them (*L'étranger* in particular, as the text of *La nausée* has never seemed to me to be as substantial) they effect me as powerfully as ever.

At the beginning of Camus' narrative, having as yet only been superficially aware of those few drowsy headlands which we (as Sartre did) assume to be part of the inconsequential flow of an inattentive humanist, we have the startling sensation of having penetrated a consciousness turned exclusively outwards, an uncomfortable highly paradoxical feeling since that consciousness would have no interior, no 'inside', affirming its existence only by the moment—without continuity—in so far as (and in the very movement with which) it projects itself constantly outwards.

In a short essay written about the same time, it's again Sartre who, to illustrate Husserl's thought, explains to us that if we

119

carelessly entered into such a consciousness we would be unceremoniously cast out in broad daylight, abandoned in the middle of the road, amidst the world's dry dust, in its blinding light ...(I'm quoting from memory which is totally justified by the wilfully subjective nature of my present undertaking.) Do we not recognise, as if it were deliberate, the Algerian setting of our opening pages: the coach ride to the Asylum at Marengo, the long walk to the cemetery, the stifling heat on the Mitidja plains scorched by the Summer? Dry dust and blinding light, this is certainly Meursault's physico-metaphysical universe.

By an astonishing stroke of luck (or genius), Camus will then transform this native landscape, which for him is the place of 'familiarity' par excellence, into the very metaphor for 'strangeness', or more accurately into its 'natural' objective correlative. And the book's power comes initially from the *amazing* presence of the world through the words of a narrator who is outside of himself, a tangible world in which we totally, unhesitatingly believe 'as if it were there' or even better still: we believe in it so firmly that we might forget its lesson: the sudden gratuitous appearance of things under the gaze of a blank consciousness strikes us with such crude violence that we hardly notice that it's the perfect, almost didactic representation of the phenomenological experience, according to Husserl.

Albert Camus and the sun ...Albert Camus and the Mediterranean beaches...The land where the orange trees of the Goethean soul bloom can't be far away—so we assume—steeped in Kantian humanism and tranquil happiness. It certainly is the same serene sky, the same inviting sea, the same light, the same heat gently ripening the golden fruit ...Not at all! Suddenly everything has changed. It's even as if each of these signs has been inverted: we are poles apart. Certainly Algeria isn't Tuscany, not even the Campagna, but above all Goethe, a product of the Nordic mists, had made his Italy into the ideal climate where reason flourished. For him the Mediterranean civilisation, despite its parched soil and bright light, was the maternal womb, the damp, warm hollow in the shade of the law, the natural cradle of moderation, harmony, eternal wisdom ...And now here everything (light, drought, sun, heat) has become oppressive, extreme, inhuman, charged with menace.

Soon things do in fact deteriorate, while Meursault is revealed as the opposite of a blank consciousness; and it's precisely this that is from the beginning betrayed by the few anthropocentric metaphors that escaped his vigilance. He does indeed have an inner consciousness, a full, transcendant inner world in the Kantian mode: hidden within is pure reason *a priori*, which has always been there since it preceded any lived experience. What this consciousness needed was to feed off the external world, devour it day by day, digest it and in the end itself become the world, leaving nothing outside.

Through a sort of moral puritanism Meursault claims to refrain in his turn from providing any social reproduction of ready-made feelings, conventional speech and codified laws. But it's against his innermost self that he then has to accomplish the inverse movement of alimentary appropriation: he has to purge his soul relentlessly by casting himself out as if he were bailing out a boat that's filling with water, unburdening it by throwing overboard the meagre treasures stored in its hold.

Now he does this without realising that this evacuation (this expulsion) day by day adds to the superfluity outside, while at the same time it gradually creates a vast empty space within his unfortunate consciousness, maintained at the cost of an increasingly ruinous expenditure of energy, a space that's caving in an all sides. And now we see that this sort of emptiness is merely a parody of a true Husserlian consciousness which wouldn't have any inside, and never would have; it would be—in the movement of its projection outwards—simply the source of the phenomena which make up the world, whereas Meursault is preparing for a tragic fight to the death against this world.

We soon have an intimation of the inevitable drama: this fake outsider will be cornered and resort to some desperate measure: a shout, an attack, an absurd crime. Or rather, it will happen on its own, outside his control (what an irony!) for it's the sun, the dry dust, the blinding light that will commit the crime through his paralysed hand.

The four brief shots in mid-afternoon on the deserted, scorching beach burst like an anticipated implosion. The dangerous imbalance between the outside world that's too full and this emptied consciousness—not devoid of interiority as it would like to be, but on the contrary, undermined from within by the vacuum it has created—could only explode: in a fraction of a second the soul, drained, will reabsorb the whole of the world it rejected, with its adjectives, emotions, passions, madness, and is instantly smashed to pieces.

And immediately after the implosion I wake up on the other side of the world in which I've been living until now: I who claimed only to be able to exist by projecting myself outwards, am now by a cruel topological inversion of space, locked in a prison cell, something closed, cubic, white probably, and there's nothing inside these four walls which are now the only outside I'll have; no furniture, people, sand, sea, nothing but me.

What a strange caricature of the maternal womb this sunless hole is, a waiting-room for my impending execution, for I am well aware that I will be condemned to death for reasons of implosion. I look out of a small, inaccessible square opening high up in the wall with a new intensity and an emotion that I now accept; I catch every single shade of colour in the sky at nightfall; and I 'devour with my eyes' every detail of this beautiful clear sky turning imperceptibly pink, mauve, jade green. This time I recognise Latin tranquillity: on the other side of my absurd window (the side that's lost forever) Goethe beckons to me once more.

If I'm not contemplating the sky, because its too dark at night or because of the glare at mid-day, I try and remember: I attempt a detailed reconstruction of my old room; taking my time I persist in trying to rediscover all the objects, their exact position and real state, their shape, colour, material, as well as the minute flaws or accidental, inexplicable surface damage: paint flaking off, scratches in the woodwork, small dents in metal, odd crockery—everything that made them into real things and not abstract models. Often, looking for instance for the exact shape of a few millimetres of veneer missing from the corner of a piece of furniture, I think I'm maybe making things up, but I can

122

see everything so clearly, so distinctly that I can't tell the difference. And sometimes I even think that what is most real is precisely what I've made up.

Then when I feel like a rest, I take another look at my press cutting. It's a news item from a very old newspaper: doubtless a sexual crime, (but for decency's sake the editor couldn't be more explicit) a crime against a little girl by a man called Nicolas Stavrogin. Both the reconstruction of the room and the newspaper clipping that's almost illegible because of the folds in the poor quality paper are now in my third novel *Le voyeur*. As for the chipped veneer, if I remember rightly, I've already mentioned it in this present work.

But in my prison cell where I have all the time in the world to think over these problems, I sometimes suspect I must have confused Henri de Corinthe with the Marquis de Rollebon whom I mentioned a few pages before in connection with *La nausée* because of certain similarities in their obscure political adventures. This muddle is doubtless because of Comte Henri's mysterious travels—as my father always called them—in Russia and Germany towards the end of the Thirties, or the beginning of the Forties, some hundred and fifty years after Rollebon's.

Exactly like Stavrogin in Dostoevsky's novel, Corinthe is almost always on the move during that frenzied, brutal time. His uncertain activities take place on the sidelines and we only know fragments that are difficult to piece together; they are mostly from the accounts (sometimes consistent, sometimes contradictory, in most cases with no obvious connection between them) of a third party and many of these people didn't themselves know him personally. It was obviously in the interest of at least one of these unreliable or frankly suspect witnesses, Alexandre Zara, to lie about his possible relations with other international agitators: we do in fact now know that he was himself a Nazi agent who had worked in London and that after he was captured by British counter espionage at the end of the war, he always attempted to cover his tracks, not hesitating to compromise innocent people, particularly influential ones.

In September 1938 Corinthe is in Berlin—there seems no doubt about that—and he meets two prominent figures close to the chancellor, one of them several times. But the German newspapers of the time are already presenting him as an invalid who has to spend most of the day resting. Rumours run rife, taken up by the press, about a sword duel where he was allegedly so badly wounded in the throat that surgeons despaired for his life. The twenty-fourth of that month a reporter visits him at the Astoria hotel, near Wilhelmstrasse, to interview him about extreme right wing factions in Europe; he finds himself, he says, in the presence of a much weakened man 'wearing a thick white bandage round his neck which could be hiding a brace or even some chance wound or malignant tumour'.

However, in the beginning of October (so, just after the Munich agreements on the Sudeten territories), he's in Prague, arriving on the evening of the seventh (from Crakow by train, it's thought) that is, scarcely a few hours before the blowing up of a goods train from Germany which seriously damaged the famous Wilson Station at the top of Wencelas Avenue in the centre of the city. The presence of such a convoy in a railway station essentially reserved for passengers was already problematical. The numerous improbabilites in the inconsistent offical communiqués published in the following days by the Czech authorities gave rise to the most preposterous suppositions. And still today, almost half a century later, the nature of the material being transported by train as well as the technical cause of the disaster, which seems to almost everyone to have been treason, are disputed among those historians who are interested in these preliminaries to the Second World War.

In any case, Corinthe's presence on the scene hardly seems coincidental; in a hand-written letter to an unknown recepient, drafted in all probability on the very day of the catastrophe—(it was found after the allied victory in the archives of the secret police in Dresden), Comte Henri gives a detailed inventory of damage caused to railways in impersonal terms that distinctly suggest he's writing a report of a mission, although it's not possible to grasp its exact nature or for whom it was carried out.

In any case, the possibly friendly, anyway cordial relations between Henri de Corinthe and Conrad Henlein (head of the pro-Nazis in Sudetenland and North Bohemia) seem to be confirmed by a photograph taken in Paris less than two years before, at the time of the inauguration of the German pavillion at the International Exhibition of 1937. The two men are perfectly recognisable, laughing together as they raise their glasses among a group of German and French notables.

I was fifteen and I remember with bitterness how that day produced the feeling of some grotesque disaster in France: on the date set for the opening of the exhibition only two pavillions were ready: one for Hitler's Germany and one for Soviet Russia which were both curiously alike. The architecture was massive, square, imposing, decorated with giant statues—whose pompous sobriety today defines the fascist style for us; they stood opposite each other on the right bank of the Seine, by the entrance to the Pont d'Iéna: a huge swastika facing the hammer and sickle held at arms length. Everything else from the Chaillot hill to the Ecole Militaire was nothing but a vast building-site of rubble and mud—the predictable result of recurrent strikes on the part of the Popular Front—where a few lost ministers were floundering around. The USSR and Germany alone had decided only to trust their own workmen and technicians. The comments in my family that evening can well be imagined.

And yet a few weeks later, at the beginning of the summer, I remember happy, scorching days and long delightful strolls through the exhibition that was finally finished; we went looking for shade under the trees in the unrecognisable landscape that must have been the Champs de Mars and the Quais; we sought small shady squares between the unlikely, enchanting, astonishing or simply preposterous constructions, resting a few minutes beside a fountain, drinking exotic fruit juices, nibbling highly spiced or bitter-sweet food before setting off again in search of new discoveries, always with our mother who had much more of a flare for meandering in the gardens and pavillions than my father.

Doubtless I was quite ignorant; I had a vast dreamy thirst

125

to learn as much as possible and I was ecstatic about everything. My mother, always approachable, attentive, full of plans (often fanciful) was the ideal companion on these wanderings. Afterwards we spent ages recalling an inside-out Polish house, the Tunisian *merguez* that I tasted for the first time—so delicious that they've ever since left their strong Oriental scent in my mouth—and then the unknown plants, Japanese steps, terraces, glass walls or a whole series of louvered shutters in two coloured Venezuelan hardwood, so thin they were translucent. I remember hot nights too—as if the Parisian climate had also changed for the occasion— and the bright lights, a supernatural green among the chestnut tree leaves, shedding their metallic glittering rays over this new imaginary world.

The importance of things—thin aromatic sausages or electric lights hidden in the foliage—obviously doesn't lie in their intrinsic significance but in the way they stick in our memory. And clearly, the strongest ties between people who are close to each other are above all made out of small insignificant things. So, I'm sure that throughout my childhood and long after I kept alive a dense network of tastes shared with my mother that probably came from her, but also a solid though more intangible fabric of tiny events and minute sensations that we both experienced in the same way from day to day.

I should, for instance, mention our mutual love of gardens and gardening, a marked gift for culinary invention, our fondness for making complicated detailed plans in our heads (from the simple journey from one place to another in Paris to the complete transformation of a house or neighbourhood), also a passion for pointless discussions about anything under the sun, preferably irrelevances, or even, quite simply, our remarkable tendency to waste time doing nothing. But all these are still relatively important traits, global options in a way, whereas the most precious things we shared were certainly much more modest, without the slightest universal character, so fragmentary, spontaneous, transitory that I don't think its particularly interesting to try and find the best examples today. A bluish bird feather, a scrap of silver sweet-paper, a new shoot coming up, a lemon-yellow straw in the dusty road, a red ant carrying a crumb...I could take almost any detail at random since what's essential is how you perceive them and above all how they are woven together.

My father used to say that my mother and I loved 'nooks' (he used an old fashioned slang word, or a word from the family dialect); he meant that we were less affected by some vast landscape than by some isolated, unobtrusive, somewhat marginal element: rather than the large lake viewed from the top of a mountain we preferred the fortuitous arrangement of three mossy stones beside a pool. Sometimes he gently ridiculed mother's myopia and also her nose, which he said was gigantic. But I myself had quite normal vision and I had the same tendency to look at the world from very close up so I could distinguish more and more subtle variations, even when they made no sense.

And probably, like her, I was particularly drawn to minute objects. Throughout my childhood I made myself miniature toys out of the most fragile materials. They often told me this story: one year when my parents asked me what toy I wanted to find on the twenty-fifth of December in front of the black marble fire place where we excitedly hung up our stockings the night before, I had solemnly asked Father Christmas to bring me 'spent match sticks'. Our gifts were simple, certainly, but things weren't that bad!

This time they gave me a whole assortment of thin sticks and slats in poplar wood (one or two millimetres thick) as well as a child's set of joinery tools, just like an adult's: saw, hammer, rasps and files, square, etc. with various drills. An enthusiastic builder for many months and even several years, I instantly set about building miniature houses—Roman, Etruscan or Byzantine—inspired by the 'Habitation' plates in the two volume Larousse.

I also spent whole days classifying things, putting them in small cardboard boxes, labelling them as carefully as if they were show cases in a museum and laying them neatly on beds of cotton wool: bits of lobsters and sea urchins I'd taken apart and carefully cleaned. Also various collections of things of no value: thorns from different bushes, beetles with their multicoloured metallic wing cases; fossil nummulites split in two along the circumference to show the spiral chamber where the protozoa once lived; fragile, diaphanous shells, with rose petal whorls, picked up on the beach, dried and chosen for their delicate pearly coloured flesh.

Yes, O.K. I'm coming to it: I did also have two china dolls a few centimetres high which I used to dress and undress. They were obviously not baby dolls but already little girls. I was doubtless faithful to them for a very long time, as—with their limbs attached, naturally—they had the benefit of my first erotic practices. In fact my perverse tastes manifested themselves at such an early age that when I think about it they seem to precede any heterosexual awareness: I happily dreamed of the massacre of my school mates (and the primary schools weren't mixed), but the ones I thought were ugly, or I didn't like, were summararily disposed of, simply to get rid of them, whereas the graceful bodies with their pretty, delicate faces had the right to long drawn out torture sessions tied to the chestnut-tree trunks in the playground.

Meticulous, sadistic, thrifty as well, I here admit in front of good old Doctor Freud that from very early on I'd acquired these three attributes out of which he created one of his favourite complexes. And, for the benefit of his present or future descendants I'd also like to point out to all and sundry that I sucked at the maternal breast till I was over two years old and, able to walk and to talk almost fluently, I could demand this exclusive nourishment with no ambiguity in words that have remained legendary in the family: 'Not cup milk, mummy's milk.'

My mother was always meticulous and patient even when performing the most trivial tasks and was also able to transform most of them into games. As for her love of very small things, it was so well known in the family and among friends that everyone liked to bring her something back from their travels. There's still a show case in Kerangoff with miscellaneous objects on display: from Cevenol kitchen equipment only a few millimetres in size to Japanese figures made out of grains of rice.

But any issue of an explicitly carnal nature, or even merely implicitly erotic, radically separated us. Very early on I'd sensed there was no possible meeting ground on that subject. And I who told her everything was instinctively silent about my cruel imaginary scenes and my nocturnal pleasures. Whenever anyone mentioned sexual complications of any kind—apart from lesbian relations (romantic or otherwise, I don't know) which she's always seemed to me to treat indulgently—they were (in her words at least) smilingly denounced as more degrading than anything else, and maybe she felt the same about so-called normal coition.

Nevertheless, I am convinced that she had no trace of puritanism or prudery. Her relations with the world were openly sensual, leaving no room for hypocritical disguise. Besides, she talked about everything very freely for that time; for instance laughing at the sodomist propaganda which—apparently—one of her friends from the past went in for, or else giving this kind of advice to a young girl: 'There are boys you sleep with but whom you don't marry'— a verdict delivered with the authority she assumed when judging people on first meeting, categorically and definitively.

Today I tell myself that she must have felt a much greater complicity when it was a question of female pleasure; she always more or less accused male sexual pleasure of being violent, simplistic and crude. Having read *La nausée* because of my interest in the book, she pronounced an irrevocable judgement on Roquentin because he asked his girl friend (I've never checked this in the text) for oral favours. She always had such immediate and passionate contact with everything real or imaginary that a hero in a book—albeit the messenger of a new metaphysic— seemed first and foremost someone with whom she did or didn't wish to associate. My mother was actually saying to me: your friend Roquentin is a repulsive guy, don't bother to invite him here again! She was very excitable. I answered, smiling: 'You are overdoing it a bit!' But quite soon I gave up trying to make her see my way of reading literature.

And yet could my judgement be clouded by a sense of personal guilt influencing my impressions of her reaction to this disturbing realm of eros? Anyway, her attitude to men and their fantasies seemed all the more striking since she protected with an all embracing tenderness the mating of all animals, birds or cats, even when certain tomcats manifested their strongly sado-erotic tendencies in front of her. As with all my manuscripts when I began writing, my mother was the first to read *Le voyeur*. When she'd finished she said to me: 'I think it's a remarkable book, but I would have preferred it not to be written by my son'—as I've already mentioned.

At an international conference a few years ago I heard a well-known film director—Indian or Egyptian, I forget—explain to an audience of spell-bound film buffs that his main concern when filming a scene could be summed up by the simple question: 'Will my mother understand, will she like what I'm doing?' Telling stories to your mother who's also the supreme judge—after all why not? It's as good a criterion as any. But I probably didn't write my novels for mine, nor produce my films to please her. Would that then mean I was working against her? I don't think so either, although my apparent predilection for dispassionate narrative may be seen as a sort of defence reaction against the too fervent subjectivity with which she expressed her feelings.

And yet if you took that point of view you could just as well say that I started to write (and then make films) in that objective way out of a distrust of my own inclinations or even in open conflict with myself. For I did share with my mother the questionable taste for a whole literature of passion and despair—I've already mentioned it—whereas my father in a rage interrupted our over impassioned reading of *Jude the Obscure* by leaping up and throwing the book on the floor and we had great difficulty stopping him from trampling it underfoot, in a healthy reaction of self defence. As for me, I cried my eyes out reading the harrowing ending of *Fortune Carée;* and it was no consolation when, in an attempt to pacify me they kept saying that it wasn't a true story, that the author had made it all up on purpose to catch me out.

So, even if I do work against many of my inclinations, it's

130

for my self alone that I write and make films and it does amuse me when an erudite film critic writes an article explaining to his countless fans (condemning me yet again) that Robbe-Grillet hasn't yet understood, sadly, the specifically 'popular' nature of the seventh art (which wouldn't be one, anyway, since there's only subjective art). And now this book, which seems to be meant for the reader or even the critic—I'm not at all sure that I'm not, as usual, the unique target. You always create for yourself even if you do dream of world-wide sales or full houses.

Unconsciously I might have made up stories to control my increasingly compulsive criminal fantasies (the ghost of the Marquis de Sade coming to pull me out of bed) but, at the same time, to counter on the other hand, the over-sensitivity of a tender hearted, backward, grizzling child upset for days on end by negligeable, often imaginary sorrows dwelt on till a lump comes to the throat, the eyes fill with tears—especially if they're to do with very young women or little children. An example suddenly comes to mind that's been hidden away for at least half a century...

Our father is scarcely more than five or six years old. It's in the Haut Jura. The gang of friends, boys and girls, have decided to make a cake and each one has to bring some implement or ingredient. My dear father in his school smock goes off happily to meet the others, carefully holding the precious lump of butter that his mother has given him for this important occasion. But once they've met up again the novice pastry cooks quarrel. They won't make anything after all. And the little child returns all alone, toddling along in the sun on the same winding path between the meadows, stumbling blindly, sniffling, desperately disappointed, his heart suddenly bursting with all the misery in the world, the clumsily wrapped, useless lump of butter gradually melting in his hands. Why did they tell us this trivial mishap? Why was he so excessively distressed that he still remembers the whole episode forty years later?

Naturally it's Catherine who moves me most easily to pity, vain tenderness and foolish indulgence now, since she's my wife and my children too and I feel totally responsible for her, for her happiness—whereas she gets along very well on her own; I feel guilty if she suffers, even if it's nothing to do with me. And so our life together seems to me to be strewn with minute, sad stories when I'm suddenly once more completely at a loss, clumsy, beside myself in the face of the inconsolable, heartrending fits of despair which will still scar my memory when Catherine has long forgotten them.

For example: soon after our marriage; we are living in Boulevard Maillot in the new flat that we owe to Paulhan's discrete kindness. I've been taking a nap in the afternoon, as I often do since my 'colonial' stint a long time ago, while my child wife has gone to fetch some net curtains from the cleaners. When I emerge from my room I see her stricken face and meet her eyes swollen with barely suppressed tears. In response to my anxious questions, unable to contain herself any longer she bursts into painful, harrowing sobs and as spasms of grief contort her features she can hardly manage to murmur the irrevocable: 'My curtain, they've torn it.'

A banal laundry incident, sure, but at the sight of the hideous, jagged tear in the almost brand new muslin I already share wholeheartedly in her misery. And then, above all, it's Catherine and I love her and that's no help to her at all, and she looks like a little waif abandoned among ruins ...It's the time when it seems hard to believe that she's no longer a child but really a young woman. When she took her wedding dress to be cleaned before the ceremony (a private, civil ceremony, don't worry) because the dressmaker had delivered it slightly soiled after making it—the same cleaner (who didn't know her then) took pains to explain to her, as if to a child who won't understand, 'Next time dear, you must tell your mummy that you have to unpick the lining first.'—'Yes Madame,' Catherine answered, without turning a hair.

Faced with the salesman who rings the bell, and, disconcerted by her size and appearance, asks if there's no one in, she quite simply says 'No, no one's in' and shuts the door, locking it for safety. In Hamburg two years later, after a lecture I've just given at the French Institute, our consul general decides to say

132

something nice to this pretty young girl lost among all those grown ups: 'Don't you get bored, Mademoiselle, accompanying your daddy on lecture tours?' But this time she replies with her most winning smile: 'He's not my daddy Monsieur, he's my husband!' The poor diplomat doesn't know where to put himself while she and I, accomplices, are delighted by his mistake.

Actually, age hasn't got anything to do with it, nor has the face or character. After so many years together setting up homes or travelling the world, despite her very independent life with all kinds of friends and despite her fortunate self-sufficiency Catherine is nevertheless, still my little girl. And so I'll end this insistent sentimental passage with a very recent scene.

I've been alone in Mesnil for several days; I'm waiting impatiently for her to come back as arranged that evening. She arrives at last, very late at night as usual. I don't know what to do to celebrate her return, despite her obvious irritation when I confess my irrational anxiety; when I wait for her the whole evening at a window on the first floor, watching for her headlights through the trees at the entrance to the grounds, I invariably imagine that she's got lost, that goodness knows what's happened to her, like my mother in the past when I came home later than the time she'd set or reckoned I'd be back.

And then because I'm clumsy opening a cupboard or because by bad luck things are in an awkward place, I knock over a transparent glass demi-john, (made into a lamp), on the corner of the cherry wood sideboard in the kitchen. The fragile sphere smashes to smithereens on the flagstones. Catherine cries out like a wounded bird, her voice incredulous, beseeching: 'Oh! No!' In the ensuing silence she stands quite still for a moment contemplating the disaster at her feet; then she leans down slowly and gently picks up some of the larger sharp splinters, fragile as a dream, as if there were still hope of sticking them together again. But soon, discouraged, she drops them back on the floor and murmurs in a subdued voice as desolate as lost happiness: 'It was like a big blue bubble...'

It wasn't a very valuable object, only an old hand-blown bottle from the past that she'd found in the cellar miraculously intact despite having no protective casing, when she was sorting out

133

the house in Bourg-la-Reine after her grandmother's death. But I knew she was very fond of it—as a souvenir from her childhood maybe—because of its extremely delicate glass and very pale bluish colour, whereas most of the old demi-johns are made of coarser greenish material.

There you are. Irreparable. I hug Catherine with all my strength, trying to console her. I know very well I can't help. In the night that now tastes of ashes, I reverently tidy away the remains of the demi-john, placing it in the mortuary hollow of a cardboard box—a piece of evidence (I say as an excuse)—in the hope, who knows, of one day finding another just like it in some country junk-shop. But up to now I still haven't found anything like it.

I've often been asked why there's so much broken glass in my films from *Marienbad* to *La belle captive* long before the accident I've mentioned here I usually answer that it makes an interesting noise (a series of cristalline sounds covering a broad spectrum and enabling Michel Fano to introduce various transformations with the help of a synthesiser) and also that the fragments strewn around catch the light prettily...

But I'm perfectly aware that this kind of explanation is never satisfactory. On the other hand, I don't see any affective relation between the sound images I've been able to produce as I constantly re-orchestrate new combinations and this bitter episode in the family history (which, I repeat, happened much later). And yet there *must* be a connection. Anyway, now the link has been made structurally: through the rapprochement that's just taken place as I write.

As for the desperate feelings of paternal love—needless to say incestuous—that I'd felt for Catherine from our first meeting, my mother was surprised(doubtless alarmed) that they could coincide with the writing of *Le voyeur* in which a precocious little girl played quite a different role. But in this case, on the contrary, the connection's obvious. Since the novel that she found shocking is still, nevertheless, loving, limitless, extravagant.

134

Le voyeur was published also by Editions de Minuit in the spring of 1955, substantial extracts being printed at the same time in two successive issues of the *Nouvelle NRF* which had just appeared. Unlike what happened with *Les gommes*, which passed virtually unnoticed two years before, only attracting the attention of a few rummagers such as Barthes or Cayrol, the moment it appeared the new book caused a small scandal from which it benefited: there were staunch supporters and passionate detractors ready with their insults—just what's needed in Paris to make a name in the world of letters. I owed this sudden spotlight mostly to Georges Bataille and the *Prix des Critiques,* an important award at the time due to the prestigious jury and to the recent winners: Camus and Sagan.

The prize was awarded in May at a meeting of literary experts where violent enmity seemed the rule. I had Bataille, Blanchot, Paulhan etc., on my side and against me there were all the influential Academy critics who wrote articles for the daily papers and literary periodicals— what was then called the 'ground floor' because their articles took up the whole bottom third of the page. After the modernists had won a narrow victory in a battle that raged for several hours, the furious losers instantly gave me the best publicity a writer could possibly dream of: Henri Clouard kicked up a row and resigned from the jury while the gentle Emile Henriot in *Le Monde* demanded that I be committed to a lunatic asylum or to the court of summary jurisdiction, if not the Assizes!

All this uproar, plus the enthusiastic praise of Roland Barthes in *Critique* and Maurice Blanchot in the *NRF* (tributes which were, by the way, incompatible: Blanchot only seeing the sexual crime and Barthes blithely ignoring it) obviously gained me a few readers and a budding notoriety. Albert Camus and André Breton gave me warm encouragement. *L'Express* opened its columns to me for a series of articles on 'Literature today' which were the origin of the 'manifestos' subsequently published in the *NRF* and later the essay *Pour un nouveau roman.*

Also, this is the time when Dominique Aury finds it imperative that the letter I received from Gaston Gallimard a few years before rejecting *Le régicide* should go missing. It was a short typewritten note on headed notepaper. Although I'm not sure of the exact wording I remember its contents perfectly—the rough meaning was: your story is interesting but as it doesn't meet the need of any kind of public we feel it's pointless to publish it. A few cyclostyled copies would be sufficient for its circulation. However, Jean Paulhan, who's always liked eccentrics, has taken note of it and will get in touch with you should the occasion arise...

When Paulhan's valuable assistant asks me to lend her this document on the pretext of finding out who wrote it, it doesn't occur to me that they must have a copy on file in the Rue Sébastien-Bottin. So I hand over the original without taking a photocopy, which wasn't normally done at that time anyway. And when I ask for my letter back a few weeks later, Dominique Aury is thunderstruck: What letter? Gallimard can't have rejected *Un régicide* since they'd never had it to read! Isn't that so Jean?—Really Dominique, you remember: I gave you the manuscript personally when you were living at the Cité universitaire.—Oh yes I remember; but I handed it over to the Editions Robert Machin, and they did immediately agree to publish it... sadly, just before they went bankrupt, etc.

I say no more. I'm stunned—it's all a bit much. Paulhan flashes his legendary smile at me, radiating innocent candour—amused, benevolent, charming and inscrutable: impossible to say whether this is the genuine surprise of an old man who has very conveniently forgotten all about it or the jubilation of the kid who's just pulled off a successful trick. Natalie Sarraute used to say: He's Talleyrand and Dominique Aury's Fouché! And yet I was fond of them both and admired Paulhan, the man and his work, and still do. I also appreciated the inimitable way in which he who never hesitated to help his protegés suddenly made them ill at ease (for example, systematically praising such and such a detail in my books ...which didn't exist). As for Dominique Aury, it was she—and this she willingly admits—who passed *Un régicide* over to Georges Lambrichs after Gallimard rejected it, while I was looking after my banana trees in the Antilles. It's she, in a way, who introduced me to Editions de Minuit and I'm very grateful to her. Besides, this vanishing trick with a letter thought to be compromising was actually rather flattering to me.

136

It's also that summer that I met Bruce Morrissette, American University expert on fake Rimbauds, who'd come to Paris from Saint Louis, Missouri for the publication of a huge, scholarly tome devoted to *La chasse spirituelle* (astute analysis which managed to cause a misunderstanding between him and André Breton as well as Maurice Nadeau and all those whose names were rashly mixed up in this amusing affair). Morrissette, having heard of my book on the radio by chance, wanted to meet me ...We immediately became friends. Intelligent, highly cultured, excited by all forms of modernism (I think it was he who first told me about Robert Rauschenberg who, on his debut, attracted attention by rubbing out a very beautiful pencil drawing by his elder De Kooning—as a pictorial gesture). Morrissette also had a sense of humour, rather a rare find among professors of literature; he felt that works of art are made for fun, they are the 'Sunday of life' predicted by Hegel.

Two or three years later, when Morrissette was back in France, he asked to be invited to Brest to the maternal home in Kerangoff which I had talked to him about. The whole family welcomed him with open arms, as is their way; my mother always offering hospitality to distant relatives and passing foreigners with an old fashioned liberality that I unfortunately haven't inherited from her. For my part, I made the effort to take my American friend around in order to introduce him to what I thought motivated his visit: the cliffs, dunes, heaths and sandy beaches among the rocks that had influenced my Breton childhood and were transposed as the setting for *Le voyeur*. But, apart from the megalithic monuments we came across on our travels, he scarcely seemed interested in the landscape of Léon.

On the other hand, at home he readily talked with my mother about everything under the sun. I thought he was merely being polite. After a few days he told me he was going to leave, assuring me that his stay had been very productive: he'd found what he was looking for. I asked him what that was. Bruce Morrissette answered me very simply: before devoting himself entirely to my work he wanted to be sure that I was a genuinely great writer;

137

now, geniuses have of necessity had exceptional mothers; he now knew that mine was! I must add that it was quite courageous of him to take a gamble so early on, on the work of a novelist who was just starting out, as it's only in the Sixties—and partly doubtless due to him—that I become a star topic in the universities on the other side of the Atlantic.

Was our sainted mother—as we often called her—'exceptional'? Of course at home this formed part of the family credo. But we all tended to think we were exceptional. Besides who isn't the minute you look more closely at them? It's from the acute consciousness of a sense of individuality that the clan spirit originates. However, it must be said that my mother generally made a very strong impression on those who met her. The daughter of the Olgiatti lady (whom I've already mentioned with regard to our education) called my mother 'godmother', although there was no reason to, since she hadn't been given the Christian name nor the baptismal name Yvonne, and she used to repeat admiringly: 'You are astonishing!' This emphatic apostrophe was part of our folklore.

This was very rich and consisted of all kinds of stories about her daily life which were progressively distorted as the stuff of legend until they were unrecognisable. So my mother, it was said, long before the 1914-18 War insisted on converting the back of the small grocery shop in the Rue de Recouvrance that her mother managed in the first years of this century or right at the end of the last, while Grandfather Canu was on active service … The grocery and the house it was in had already disappeared long ago, destroyed by the bombing in 1945, as had the old Rue de la Porte, when the bulldozers had levelled and straightened out poor Brest after the Second World War. But it would take more than that to stop our mythical mother solving certain subtle problems of partitions and inconvenient passageways.

There was also the famous 'bus scene'. In a traffic jam near *Printemps* our mother allegedly pushed my sister and I in front of a bus as it was moving off. As her children shrank back terrified, she apparently jeered at such a vulgar instinct for self-preservation, declaring in a loud voice that anyway 'it's better to die young'. Another time, in the only room of a spartan inn in the Arrée mountains where all four of us were staying on one of our walking tours across the Brittany interior (*ar coat* in Breton), I had a violent attack of indigestion in the middle of the night. Our mother, all of a tremble, considering that her husband whom she's woken with a start is being too slow to light a candle, leapt towards him brandishing a large knife, ready to strike him! This episode was referred to as 'Braspart's knife' (thus immortalising the name of the place) and my father used to recount it solemnly in tragic Racinian accents, to any one who'd listen, his wife having this time turned into 'the bloody Athalie'.

The chronicle also contained less extravagant, more likely if not truthful tales concerning in particular my mother's incredible faculty for forgetting the time, that is for losing time (though I'm certainly not the best one to reproach her); this meant that she would invariably arrive anywhere late and with perfect equanimity serve meals when everyone at home had gone to bed, or the guests had long since left with empty stomachs to catch the last metro. My grandmother would say to her; 'My poor child, you're on the road to ruin!' And I can in any case, guarantee the authenticity of the ritual 'watercress soup' phenomenon which took place at regular intervals.

When it was already very late in the evening my mother would begin to wash a bunch of watercress for dinner which her husband had brought back after work. Soon she would notice that among the stems tied with string or raffia were hidden a mass of aquatic insects, molluscs, worms or fresh water shellfish such as water scorpions, backswimmers, miniature leeches, lymnaea, planorbid. There were lots of gammaridae, a kind of minute amphipoda shrimp which we wrongly called daphnid and we were particularly fond of because of the way they wiggled as they swam about.

Mother immediately began to gather up all the little creatures that were still alive and put them into a jar with a few pieces of cress for company in order to make a miniature aquarium which I later spent hours gazing at in wonder. My father had had his coffee, garlic sausage and bread long ago; he was on his way to bed with a look of deep depression ('Joker'! my mother would say to him) and in the stricken tones of a prophet preaching to the unconverted he would utter this saying—I don't know where it comes from: 'And tomorrow they'll all be dead at Picard's!' Indeed the children, who were taking just as long over their homework, French composition or Latin translation, wouldn't have their soup till one or two in the morning and would have trouble getting up for school. My mother would spend the rest of the night reading the papers.

Her almost obsessive concern for all forms of animal life was certainly one of the dominant traits in her character and anecdotes abound. There was the story of the tench that my father brought home alive for a special lunch: they were instantly plunged into a bucket of fresh water and fed for several months until the summer holidays when, the day before we left, we had to set them free in the pond in Montsouris park, hiding from the keepers who would have thought, on the contrary, that we were fishing them out. The delightful fish were so used to their metal bucket that my mother, afraid of harming them as she emptied them out, had the greatest trouble coaxing them out of the bucket which was well below the surface.

I've already described the famous jackdaw who, having fallen out of some nest in Paris, had been reared and allowed to fly around in the small flat where it destroyed a great deal of wallpaper by tearing off the loose bits, until it was taken to Kerangoff and lived there for many years, half wild, half tame. Still in Paris my mother fed a young swift, weakened by the frightful parasites in its feathers, giving it a tonic for convalescents. After the bird was cured it often came to visit us through the 'study' window which we left open on purpose. On the narrow balcony we had tubs containing our two miniature gardens—one the so called 'Sahara', the other the 'Jura'—which took a lot of looking after: tidying the ragged contours, replanting, cutting back overgrown plants, raking the sandy paths, etc. In the ten centimetres of lake there were, of course, fauna from the watercress as well as minute newts—their feeding habits, pairing and the sloughing of their skin occupied us for whole afternoons on end.

But sadly a sick bat eventually died after weeks of care. It was

a tiny vespertilio weighing less than three grams. Too weak to
hibernate, suffering from a vitamin deficiency, it lived under
my mother's blouse (in what she called her pouch) next to her
warm body—to the great terror of uninitiated visitors who
thought they were hallucinating, when at table they glimpsed
between the lapels of the white collar of this impassive hostess
whose tea they were politely drinking, the creature suddenly
emerging from its hiding place to clamber awkwardly over her
breast and neck spreading its huge black silky wings.

Another much more personal memory from further back in the
past now rises out of the darkness like a bad dream. I'm very
small, very moved, very alone, lost in huge empty corridors with
very high ceilings. At last going through the imposing glass door
of the building where our classrooms are, I come out into the
fresh air and sunlight in the deserted playground with its chestnut
trees (again), their big tall gnarled trunks like blackish pillars
planted in alternate rows. It must be towards the end of my first
year in primary school in the Rue Boulard where I am pampered
by a nice smiling teacher with the transparent name of Monsieur
Clair. I still have long curly hair and a girlish look. Suddenly
taken short, I've had to ask permission to go to the lavatory.
It's already late spring as the chestnut trees have all their new
very thick green leaves.

Just where the sunlight and the shadow cast by the first tree
on the gravel meet there's a young fallen sparrow who can't fly
or stand up. Half-paralysed I hold my breath as I come down
the three sloping steps leading to the playground. The bird must
be injured, otherwise it wouldn't be dragging itself round in
circles like this. My mother would have instantly picked it up,
examined it, looked after it, disinfected its wounds, put a splint
on its broken limb ...Away from her I don't know what to do
for this fragile ball of feathers struggling and cheeping softly.

On a sudden impulse, in order to put an end to its suffering,
I put my foot on it and press. It's not a common snail. It's much
firmer and more resistant. And also, I'm afraid of hurting,
crushing this thing that's still alive. Panic stricken, I end up using

all my childish strength. It squelches under my shoe. I feel I'm committing a sordid murder. Soon I realise, terrified, that there's blood on my sole and even a bit of grey down stuck to it I can't get off as I scrape my feet on the gravel and weak at the knees, heart thumping, run to the row of toilets at the end of the playground where the stable doors will only provide a temporary barrier against the overwhelming horror I feel.

That day I can't think of anything else—as if my shoe were crushing the tiny bird's body over and over again—until school's over when I'll rush to my mother waiting for me at the school gates to tell her in floods of tears about my incomprehensible crime. Last month, near the landing stage at the lower lake in Mesnil, I deliberately crushed a young coypu under my boot (I think it's proper name is a muskrat or ondatra). The big aquatic and terricolous rodents are to be found in profusion in Normandy since the war; it's said they began to breed prolifically after the fighting and Catherine is worried when they multiply within river banks which they weaken and undermine so that the trees, among whose roots they've built their labyrinthine galleries, fall. I then had the same frightful feeling from the past and thought that the poor squashed sparrow must be a real memory and not, as is often the case, a story my parent told me afterwards.

Of course our mother taught us to read and write, count and speak properly. So the infants' classes were easy for us. Besides, although of a dreamy, reflective temperament—which is a form of laziness—I've always enjoyed learning. This is doubtless part of a longing to possess the world (to *have* in order to *be*) like collecting stamps, plants or different objects, the obsession with ordering things, the impossibility of throwing anything away, the habit of taking hundred of slides (later to be classified and arranged in boxes) in every new country I visit, or learning by heart great chunks of poetry or prose. This is a common illusion: the instinct to hoard (knowledge or anything else) is part of the will to power, that is to say, the instinct of self-preservation. Only later, much later do you realise the things you've accumulated are on the side of death.

But the essential value of knowledge for its own sake in all fields has always been one of the keystones of the family ideology inherited from the grandfathers—teachers or customs officers— whether right or left wing. Grandmother Canu kept a grocery shop (which she didn't own) in a poor neighbourhood, but she had her school certificate.

Today still I have this appetite for learning, above all if it involves an intellectual effort or an effort of memory. And I find one of the attractions of the life of a university lecturer that I lead from time to time in America (in New York or on some campus lost in the vast States with their legendary names) is that I instantly become a student again. Studious pupils (mine are usually 'graduates') discussions on theory with the other teachers, peaceful places, cosy atmosphere of the cultural ghetto, exterritoriality (out of my country, out of time), all this gives me once more the eager, ambitious and gratuitous freedom of adolescence, when there's still a whole life time of learning ahead. I discover, fill in the gaps, reread closely taking notes, I go to the library for one or another of the heavy seminal works I've always, through lack of time or energy, put off reading till later.

I also try to restore a faith in culture in those of my students who have lost faith, I rehabilitate intellectual pleasure, the primacy of the mind and even, why not, élitist pride. In the past, in our simple home, we weren't ashamed to say : *odi profanum vulgus et arceo*. And I passionately condemn the mindless evenings spent in front of the 'telly' and the herd like consumption of the latest pulp best-seller, as well as the costly tripe launched by the vast mass media circus of the Californian film industry, where the most foolish gag weighs a ton, not to mention what they do with the disciplines that are already pretty heavy like psychoanalysis, boy scout ethics and social realism.

But I have to be careful over there too. If I say outright that the majority of Hitchcock's or Minelli's films are simply standard, more or less well-made products, I will doubtless either be accused of my well-known delight in being provocative or of resentment at their world-wide success both in the press and with the public.

143

So, I was a gifted pupil and enjoyed studying but— hereditary taint or infectious illness caught in my cradle—I was also always behind with my work (things haven't changed much since) so much so that a bad conscience has always been my daily lot. At four-thirty in the morning at the sound of the milk man unloading his heavy metal churns, then the musical clanging racket as he piled the empties onto the big open vehicle pulled by two draught horses outside the dairy opposite, my sister and I were very often still working under the lamp, one on each side of the double desk; the arrival of the milk was, however, the signal setting a fateful deadline that couldn't be ignored, even if the French composition or Greek prose wasn't finished.

Homework given in late, lessons learned at the last minute (brushing the tree trunks from one end of the boulevard to the other, without stepping on the iron grills was a powerful charm against being questioned in class, while you only needed one tree—preferably with a smooth bark—if you said a magic spell as you touched it, a spell I still use from time to time to calm all sorts of fears), exercise books copied out in neat writing but never handed in on time, the gaps gradually widening as the school year went on etc.—all this meant that the results weren't always praised by the teachers.

When they were plainly mediocre my father would instantly talk of getting us an apprenticeship, since we weren't up to this needlessly costly secondary education. My mother pleaded our cause and convinced him to give us another chance for one more year. Both of us in the end came through and finished the course that was considered the most prestigious at the time: Latin, Greek, Mathematics—even with fairly good results by the time we left.

I won a state scholarship in a reputedly difficult competitive exam, and got into the Lycée Buffon as a day-boy after a memorable scene. As usual my hair was too long. Having drawn my mother's attention to this fact— she's meanwhile in a flap about the time because she's got to come with me to the principal's office for my official introduction—I hear myself answering that it won't show because I'll wear my hat (a sort of silky felt bowler that accentuates my round cheeks and dainty appearance). Good. I assume we're agreed. So there we both are formally seated opposite the florid, bald headmaster who's been fixing his little piggy eyes on me ever since we came in, while my mother's trying to distract him from her late arrival and is doing her utmost to speak highly of her offspring.

'Well anyway, here's a little boy who must be very proud of his headgear; doubtless that's why he keeps it glued to his head,' finally uttered behind his august desk the fat man with the glistening pink skin; he had taken all that time to prepare his subtle reference (I imagine) to Charles Bovary's first day at school. My mother, scandalised by my bad manners which she'd just noticed, tears the offending object from my head and the mass of carefully hidden curls come tumbling down ...We argued for years afterwards about whether she had or hadn't told me to keep my hat on in front of the headmaster.

And then—possibly the next year—there was a much more disturbing incident in which this same person plays an ambivalent part, while a tall senior master with a very black, square beard has the role of the methodical sado-paedophile; after a mysterious business of satchel swapping during gym classes he would administer sharp blows with a ruler to our naked calves during the private sessions in his den which he called 'flogging no.1,2,3,' according to the severity of the punishment. This repeated punishment for an imaginary crime whose exact nature was never explained to me and which seems to be the stuff of nightmares (sexual?) upset me for months because it was so absurd: complete absence of facts, plausibility, cause and effect, logical organisation of the predicates, in a word lack of 'reality'. Again it was my mother, this time upset by the red weals on the backs of my legs, who went to the administrative authorities to try and clear up the mystery—the whole thing, for me at least, was utterly obscure.

On the other hand, it's my father who came to my defence much later in the fifth form when I'd been expelled as a day-boy for saying 'shit' to a teaching assistant. In fact I hadn't answered him at all but only muttered a little too loudly: 'Shit, you can't even get on with your work here any more', as the cantankerous master had just forbidden me to go to my pigeon hole at the

145

back of the class to get my Latin dictionary. My father, fired once again by his anarchic-libertarian spirit, had bounded up to the stupefied headmaster and announced in no uncertain terms that he thought he'd sent his son to a lycée, not to the Jesuits or a school for the Children of Mary.

And so I continued at school as a day-boy which means without the teaching assistants or the canteen; but then we had a bit more money at home and Lina the formidable Swiss woman made me meals that were infinitely superior to the ones in the refectory. My father still took us to school every morning, our respective 'institutions' being quite near each other. He strode along, his two children trotting by his side down the Avenue du Maine, Boulevard Vaugirard and Boulevard Pasteur. From the top of the Boulevard Pasteur outlined against the sky above the trees appeared the turret roofs of the main school building the slates shining in the morning sun, intricate as a Renaissance château— which is why we baptised my lycée Schloss-Buffon, in honour of Chamisso de Boncour whose moving poem dedicated to the lost Fatherland we recited as we went down the middle of the boulevard.

All this is real, that is fragmentary, fleeting, useless, so random and so specific that any incident at any moment appears gratuitous and any life seems, after all, devoid of the slightest unifying significance. The advent of the modern novel is precisely linked to this discovery: reality is discontinuous, composed of elements juxtaposed in a random fashion, each of which is unique and all the more difficult to grasp in that they emerge in a constantly unforeseen, irrelevant, haphazard way.

Anglo-Saxon essayists trace the birth of the novel genre back to the beginning of the eighteenth century, not before, when Defoe, then Richardson and Fielding decide that reality exists in the here and now, not elsewhere in some 'better' timeless other world characterised by its coherence. Henceforth the real world is no longer ascribed to the abstract (perfect) idea of things, of which every day life was until then at best merely a pale reflection, but it's to be found in things themselves, here on earth as each

146

person sees them, hears them, touches them, feels them according to his lived experience.

Consequently, reality which lay exclusively in the general and the universal (the famous scholastic 'universals') is suddenly revealed to be so particular that it becomes impossible to slot it into categories of meaning—save at the cost of serious reductive distortions. What will from then on be called *novel,* to emphasise the novelty of the genre, will then stick exclusively to concrete (which doesn't mean objective) details, fragments related with meticulous simplicity even if this is to undermine (and certainly it soon does) the possibility of constructing an image of unity or any totality whatsoever.

Thus the coherence of the world begins to collapse. And yet the narrator's authority still seems at first to be unassailable; You could almost say that he has more authority since there's no longer any other world to describe but the very one he knows. We've come down to earth, but it's more than even a kind of man-god who's speaking. Now he is simply sticking close to small immediate things rather than lofty mediatised concepts.

It took Lawrence Sterne and Diderot for the narrative voice to claim both its total creative freedom and bold lack of authority, affirming at each twist and turn of the text with a smile of complicity: no one knows what all this means, I no more than you, and anyway what does it matter, since in any case I can invent anything? We recall the startling opening to *Jacques le fataliste* and are reminded of *L'innommable* written by Samuel Beckett nearly two centuries later.

But after that exhilarating pre-revolutionary period when the notion of truth (divine as well as human) is blithely called into question, after the chaos of bloody revolutions, regicide and so-called wars of liberation we have the inevitable back-lash: it's the bourgeoisie—monarchist and Catholic—which when all's said and done takes power in France. And the new values that they venerate demand, on the contrary, absolutely fixed meanings, the plenitude of reality, chronological and causal security, non-contradiction with no possible deviation. This is a far cry from Jacques' wanderings with their unexpected spatial dislocations, their parodoxical episodic adventures and disjointed time scheme—the clock had nonchalantly been turned back—his wanderings are certainly much farther away than they are from us now. With Balzac the coherence of the world and the narrator's authority are both pushed to the limit that had never been reached.

The 'realist' ideology is born in which the world, closed and completed in a definitive, weighty, unequivocal rigidity is entirely meaningful, where the fictional elements are classified and put into a hierarchy, where the linear plot unfolds according to the reassuring laws of reason, where the characters become types: the miserly-old-man, the young-man-of-ambition, the devoted-mother, etc. The universal comes rushing back.

And even when Balzac denounces the fragmentation of man's work and the resulting fragmentation of the whole of society and of individual consciousness (which is why the Marxist Lukàcs considers him a revolutionary writer struggling against capitalist industrialisation and subsequent alienation) he does this from the heart of a text in which, on the contrary, everything reassures the triumphant bourgeoisie: the innocent, serene continuity of the narration dispels any fear on the part of the reader of a serious (structural) flaw in the system. The undisturbed exercise of power and the annexation of the world by one class is just, necessary, since the great novelist exercises this power too, under cover of the same ideals. And, of course, the avowed subjectivity of the encyclopedist Diderot is followed by objectivity, or more accurately its mask.

Immediately, however, Flaubert appears. The first great proletarian revolt in 1848 marked the turn of the century. A clear conscience and fixed values have already to a large extent begun to break down. The 'we' that opens *Madame Bovary* as it closes it (for the last sentences of the book in the present indicative similarly clarify the position of the writer as very much inside the world he's describing and no longer in some empyrean of absolute knowledge)—the improbable meaningless objects such as Charles's monstrous cap (oh my lovely bowler hat!) the strange holes in the narrative which we'll come back to—all this shows that the novel is once more being called into question. And this time things will move fast.

And yet it's impossible to regard Balzac as a brief intermediary. He remains a supreme, conclusive example (hence the historical importance that must be accorded to this monumental work, even when it's so heavy it slips out of our hands); he has become a symbol of perfect ease at the centre of his meretricious system, 'realism'; yet it also has to be said that from that time this system has, despite everything, persisted to the present day; and it really is this literary trend that is still greeted with approval by the general public and by traditional criticism.

In fact from the middle of the nineteenth century two families of novelists will develop along parallel lines. There are those on the one hand who will persist—since bourgeois values always exist whether in Rome or Moscow, even if no one believes in them any more—in constructing narratives codified once and for all according to a sub-Balzacian realist ideology, with no contradictions or gaps in the meaningful plot. And on the other hand, those who will wish to explore, going further each decade, insoluble tensions, divisions, narrative aporia, fractures, voids, etc. —for they know that reality begins at the precise moment when meaning becomes uncertain.

And so, moved by the comforting familiarity of the world, I may very well act as if everything bore the face of Man and Reason (with capital letters). And in that case I'd write like the Sagans of this world, make film like the Truffauts. Why not? Or else, quite the reverse, shocked by the startling strangeness of the world, however anguished, I shall experiment with the absence from the depths of which I myself am speaking and soon I shall recognise that the only details making up the reality of the world in which I'm living are nothing but the gaps in the continuity of those ready-made meanings, all other details being by definition ideological. Now at last I am able to shift uneasily between the two poles.

Someone (I forget who) has said that *Madame Bovary,* in a complete break with the preceding half century where everything rests on plenitude and solidity, is the precursor of the *'nouveau roman'*: 'a cross roads of gaps and misunderstandings'. And

Flaubert himself writes of Emma after the famous ball which should have satisfied her fully: 'Her visit to Vaubyessard had made a gap in her life, like those great chasms that a storm sometimes hollows out of the mountains in a single night'. This theme of the void, the fault, is all the more remarkable since it will immediately reappear twice more on the very next page.

Emma is day-dreaming in front of the Vicomte's cigar case which they found on their way home. She imagines the breath of the needlewomen passing through the gaps in the stitching of the canvas stretched on its frame and the threads of coloured silk going from hole to hole, interweaving their constantly interrupted paths to form the pattern. Isn't this an accurate metaphor for the work of the modern novelist (I am Flaubert!)—on the broken thread of reality, the writing as the reading afterwards, moving from gap to gap to construct the narrative?

I'm all the more convinced of this as, twenty lines further on, Emma has just bought a street map of Paris so she can walk round the capital without leaving her room in the provinces; she traces on the paper with her fingertip multiple complex walks, stopping at the intersecting lines of streets 'in front of the blank squares indicating houses.' The author's insistent repetition of the image of an imaginary journey between 'blanks', gaps, helps us to see to what extent the identification he claimed with his heroine is in fact something quite different from a vague, insignificant whim.

It is thanks to the holes shifting about in the texture of his novel that the text lives, like a territory in a game of 'Go' which only stays alive if you are careful to leave at least one empty space, a vacant square, what the experts call an open eye, or a freedom. If, on the contrary, all the places marked out by the intersecting lines have pieces on them, the territory is dead, the enemy could seize it simply by encircling it.

Here we find one of Einstein's fundamental ideas, popularised a few years ago by Karl Popper: the scientific criterion for testing a theory, in whatever field, is not that it can be verified as correct at each new experiment but quite the opposite, that in one case at least it can be proved wrong. Thus Marxist Leninism and orthodox psychoanalysis, Popper states, are wrongly considered by their advocates to be sciences, since these disciplines are *always* right. Closed systems, they leave no space, no area of uncertainty, no doubt as to meaning, no question without an answer. Whereas science is incompatible with such a totalitarian frame of mind: it can only be living and so there must be gaps. The same thing goes for the literature that interests me.

And so Nicolas Stavrogin returns: the 'empty centre' moving ceaselessly inside *The Possessed*. He's not a devil among devils, he's the devil incarnate: the missing devil, the devil who is *lacking*. Almost always absent from the actual scene, we only know of his movements off stage, abroad, through three short fragments reported second or third hand by shady messengers who never reveal or understand their meaning. From time to time he erupts into the foreground of events; in front of astonished witnesses he then carries out some strange, unexpected act, he utters a few disjointed, inexplicable words as unintelligible to his family or to the police as to the conspirators whose chief he seems more or less to be. Everyone assumes there must be an underlying reason for his behaviour, but in vain we puzzle over the succession of riddles wantonly multiplied in his wake,—hoping to discover it.

Right at the end of the book we find today the censured chapter that the Russian editor had originally left out in case it gave offence and we no longer know where it goes, since the rest of the chapters were renumbered consecutively by the author himself, who thus destroyed the sign that revealed the lack. Consequently, in all recent editions Stavrogin, who has already died on the preceding pages, comes back to give his confession to Bishop Tikhon. In order to make his confession clearer he's even written it in a note book ...from which he tears a couple of pages at the last minute in front of the astonished bishop. And the reader, like Tikhon, will never know what was in those pages, although he guesses they're of the utmost importance.

The narrator, to conclude (as it were!) the erratic chapter thus mutilated—and by the same token the whole volume—simply makes this comment: it's a pity that Stavrogin removed the two pages in question for if he hadn't we might possibly have at last understood the meaning of his apparently incoherent behaviour

151

and life; on the other hand, as he always lied throughout his life, he must have been lying in his confession too; and doubtless he was also lying in the pages he removed from it.

I hadn't read *The Devils* when I was writing *Le voyeur*. And yet it's as if I'd wanted to reproduce the same forbidden void, the central cavity, the same silence at the heart of the novel, but this time using the void as the generative force of the whole text—which is not the case with Dostoevsky. I repeat once more that the 'blank page'' in the *Voyeur* (between the first and second parts of the narrative) which is apparently there as the tangible sign of a lack, an emphasis which I find crude, is actually merely due to simple typographical reasons: if part one had consisted of a few more lines, the page in question would have been filled—more or less-like the others.

We didn't go to the cinema very often when I was a child and so I was all the more impressed by the rare films I did see. One of them even gave me such nightmares the whole of the following month and long after that we again had recourse to the linctus of bromide. It was *The Invisible Man* with Franchot Tone, in the mid Thirties. And I still remember a few images where the invisible presence of a mad murderer was enough to agonise a little boy already far too susceptible to crimes committed by a sort of void in the continuity of the world. For example, the driver thinking he's alone on a deserted road, having at last escaped at the wheel of his car from death who's pursuing him, is strangled with his own scarf by the invisible passenger who's been hidden in the back since he left. In the end the criminal, trapped in a hut in the middle of virgin snow, tries to flee: all we see are his footsteps slowly advancing; the detectives hidden in the surrounding thickets fire; the shape of an invisible body is outlined in the snow.

Towards the end of that decade Corinthe too often talked about 'disappearing' and we didn't quite understand whether he meant running away physically, or whether he was referring to a vague metaphysical annihilation, entering some religious order for example (Christian, Buddhist or goodness knows what). At least he wasn't the kind of man to commit suicide. 'I am going', he would say. 'I'm getting the hell out ...' and sometimes he would add: 'Taking the inner path', which I think was part of a quotation from a book he'd read in his youth. Like many quixotic intellectuals of the time he was strongly impressed by the ceremonies of the National Socialist cult in Nuremberg. He made vehement, irrational speeches about the mission of the Third Reich who were fighting against the red beast prophesied by St. John in the *Apocalypse* and in a sort of frenzy he confused Hitler's grand rallies, with a production of *Parsifal* that he'd seen in Bayreuth.

A reliable witness who met him in Bavaria at that time describes him as a sort of living corpse, half-dead, a ghost. Cadaverous, or more accurately emaciated, he's sitting at his desk cluttered with papers which must be the reworked drafts of the manuscript that has disappeared today (the most esteemed of Parisian publishers could have something to do with that) which he'd been working on for ages. Although it's summer he is huddled in a sort of travelling rug, pulled up round his neck; from this fragile form emerges a gaunt face, motionless as a mummy that's just had its wrappings removed—as in the opening of the film I mentioned earlier; he has dark rings under his glazed eyes enlarged with fever, his thin lips hardly move when he speaks. He resembles the famous Impressionist painting of Edouard Manneret at his work table. Without making a gesture despite the vehemence of his language, that day he talks fanatically, crazily to his visitor about the rising tide, trailing sea-weed, gaps between the rocks where the treacherous water swirls, spindrift streaking the surface ...

I also see on rereading my notes that his son must have been a fellow student of mine at the *Institut national agronomique*. I don't know at what stage in my work I could have scrawled these few hurried sentences, which don't seem to belong anywhere. It's so long since I began to write this document about a subject that's increasingly elusive that I often find it impossible to identify the countless secret allusions scattered throughout the old sections which were written almost ten years ago. Anyway, I don't remember anything about the supposed presence of a young

Corinthe sitting beside me in the lecture halls facing Oudot and Brianchon's gawdy frescoes. I'd have to check the class lists in a college year-book.

Nothing. I can't find anything. Tirelessly I joint together the broken threads of a tapestry that at the same time unravels itself, so that the pattern can hardly be discerned. As for the pattern, I've always known that 'the real writer has nothing to say.' Moreover, my very first article on literature, published in *Critique* even before *Les gommes* came out, began with that sentence. It dealt with a novel by an unknown writer about the futile obsession with the blank page; the author (I've forgotten his name), who was then Sartre's private secretary, subsequently turned out to be the journalist on *L'Express* whose dishonest intervention concerning my air crash has already been mentioned. But the opening words of my notes on his book were considered scandalous by the editors of *Critique,* and omitted on publication. Jean Piel has always maintained that George Bataille was responsible for this curious piece of censorship, which surprises me since in the Fifties he didn't have much to do with the editing of the review.

Besides, this is Flaubert's idea once more. And here again the severance takes place in mid-century. It's been said that Balzac is the last fortunate writer, the one whose work coincides with the values of the society that nourishes him, and this is because he is the last innocent writer: He does have something to say and he hastily amasses dozens of novels, millions of pages, without appearing to ask himself any questions as to the validity of this strange, paradoxical exercise: writing the world. Flaubert, in three books that took him a lifetime to write, discovers both the terrifying freedom of the writer, the futility of claiming to express original ideas, finally the impossibility of writing which only comes from silence and which similarly moves towards its own particular silence.

Thus the novel's content (saying something new, Balzac thought) can actually only consist in the banality of what has always-been-said-before: a string of stereotypes, lacking any originality by definition. The only meanings are established in advance by society. But these 'ready-made ideas' (which today we call ideology) are, however, going to be the only possible material for the construction of a work of art—novel, poem, essay—empty architecture whose form is its only coherence. The substance and originality of the text will come solely from the organisation of its elements which are of no interest in themselves. The writer's freedom (that is, man's freedom). resides only in the infinite complexity of possible combinations. Hasn't nature constructed all living systems from the amoeba to the human brain out of a very few amino acids and only four nucleotides, which are always the same?

In *Obliques* or elsewhere I've already talked about the genesis of the film *L'Eden et après*, created out of twelve themes from the hundreds and hundreds in the modern panoply (maze, dance, *doppelgänger*, water, door, etc.) each repeated ten times but in a different order to form ten consecutive sequences, a bit like Schönberg's serial music. While we were shooting and editing the film, the physical work (plus the creativity triggered off by an infectious euphoria) constantly fed—and upset—this generative scheme whose rigidity is no longer apparent in the finished product, even to me. Initially there was no script, only a first sequence or twelve frames of an incident written in dialogue form; the one hundred and three remaining frames were produced in collaboration with the film crew, in particular thanks to the enthusiastic contribution of the chief camera man Igor Luther and the actress Catherine Jordan who soon became, on her own initiative, the star of the film.

Obviously chance immediately came into play : for instance after a mass of fortuitous incidents, we saw the improbable, miraculous appearance of the heroine's 'double', an identical twin even wearing the same clothes. As for the theme of 'blood' that had just played an important part in the first three weeks of filming in the Slovak State studios, it suddenly took on an unexpected dimension in real life.

So, we're in Bratislava at the end of August 1969. For the last six days we've been struggling to perfect the set of the Eden café: a labyrinthine system of panels inspired by Mondrian which slide on intersecting parallel rails across the whole set, the position being changed after each take and sometimes even during shooting in order to make the set even more fluid. On the Saturday evening I have the chance to go and drink a carafe of white wine after dinner in a strip-tease bar (a legacy of the Prague spring, as was my contract) so I can choose a nude extra for the following Tuesday. Catherine and my Tunisian assistant who are both tired leave soon. I stay with Catherine Jourdan (whom I just call Jourdan to avoid confusion), a young French actor and an official from the Tunisian co-production.

As we're walking back to our hotel through the deserted city about midnight, cheerful and relaxed, we make a few obviously silly jokes about a small Soviet plane which is on show opposite the Carlton, as a gesture of provocation. Having reached the main entrance to this building with its antiquated luxury (we're staying at the more modern Dévin, three hundred metres away on the Danube), a police patrol accosts us; perhaps they noticed our irreverent gestures although they were harmless enough.

Considering myself responsible for the little group I cheerfully undertake to justify our late night stroll. Besides, there isn't a curfew. The Franco-Czech film I'm making is under the official auspices of the nationalised film industry. And a few days before I'd even been given the local decoration which corresponds to our *Arts et Lettres*. But as I only know a few words of the language I make the mistake of muddling through in German and doubtless they take us for Austrian tourists (Vienna is a few kilometres away on the opposite bank of the river) who've come to live it up on the cheap thanks to their abominable, capitalist hard currency. To make matters worse my hair is yet again too long to be that of a good average Communist, and I'd forgotten to shave that morning (I didn't have a beard at that time, only a moustache, also Western).

Two of the policemen are in uniform, the three others in plain clothes. All five have crew cuts, shaven necks, but they're very red in the face, probably drunk. It is the very day of the anniversary of the entry of the Warsaw pact troops, who had come precisely to put an end to the general licence and the authorities

156

are afraid that commemorative demonstrations may be held; and so rumour has it that they've doped their most loyal troops as some of the more excitable ones are obviously spoiling for a fight. One of the plain clothes policemen asks for my papers: I hand them over.

But at the same moment his neighbour who has a sort of knuckle duster on his right hand, brandishing a cannister in his left, squirts a few jets of paralysing gas into my face. He immediately starts punching me in the jaw. Completely dazed, I lean back against the wall of the Carlton while—I was told later—flailing about with my arms as if I were drowsily chasing insects away in slow motion; of course not warding off the well aimed blows that continue to rain down on my face. My two masculine companions watch the massacre without turning a hair, intimidated by the soldiers. And it is Jourdan who intervenes: she thrusts her delicate face in front of mine to protect me, staring defiantly at my attacker. The man for a moment hesitates to disfigure this pretty girl. His armed fist falls to his side.

My identity card is returned to me in silence, as if after some banal routine check. And we're left to go on our way undisturbed. It all happened as if in a dream, with no explanation, no shouting, no confusion. I almost feel like saying no violence: the world seemed wrapped in cotton wool, including the metal weapon whose repeated blows on my jaw, doubtless anaesthetised by the gas, I hardly felt. But when I get to my room I realise by Catherine's expression that I must be seriously injured.

I look at myself in the bathroom mirror: I have two broken teeth in the upper jaw on the left, another that's loose and deep cuts above and below the mouth; three quarters of my white shirt is red from collar to waist (lip injuries bleed a lot); the shape of the blood stains ironically recall a cruel scene filmed in the studio that morning. Having gradually recovered with the help of towels soaked in cold water I then remember the shape of the vaporizer the policeman used: it curiously resembled a small object (used to scare off trouble-makers) which is already on one of the reels of my film (but that sequence was finally only seen in an anagrammatic version for television whose structure is random rather than sequential, called *N. a pris les dés*).

157

From dawn onwards the whole production team is in an uproar. I make the aquaintance of the free health service of so-called real Socialist countries: a party member goes everywhere with me to slip hundred crown notes to the nurses who meet me and to the surgeons who examine me or sew me up. And then the authorities are quick to reassure me: I mustn't be upset by a mere misunderstanding, the valiant guardians of law and order just didn't know who I was! This confirms my first impression: as usual this business that happened to me really didn't have anything to do with me ...

Another image which must come from the following days: the dentist leaning over me who—in a bitter profession of anti-Communist faith, strongly advises me to have the necessary denture made in France—yells in my face his diagnosis of the incisor that at first seemed to be the least damaged as he vigorously ill treats the root: 'Ah! ah! it's loose Monsieur the expert! It's loose!' he repeated in French grimacing and laughing.

I remember the close woman friend with whom my mother must have been in love (or vice versa) who was a dental surgeon in Brest. She always looked after our teeth when we were children and her gentleness and skill added to the charm of her—to us—very luxurious flat, where she played *The submerged cathedral* on an ebony grand piano. It is she who told me about the strange wound that Henri de Corinthe had on his neck: two little red holes about a centimetre apart that she found when she was taking out a wisdom tooth.

Corinthe died in Finistère a short while afterwards. My father went to his funeral, a civil funeral with an unlawful mass celebrated by an unfrocked priest, held in the open air outside the closed church door. It took place in a little town on the west coast, something like Porsmoguer-en-Plouarzel where Comte Henri lived alone at the bottom of an old gun emplacement from the time of Vauban, built into the cliff (you had to go down a stone staircase to get to the rooms); he had bought it from the estate and converted it in a very spartan fashion. So he had been excommunicated. For how long? Why? The small procession

158

stopped in a sort of church close opposite the silent bell-tower. A fine cold drizzle had been falling since the day before. It was the end of autumn. The men knelt down in their dark suits on the sodden earth. When my father described it on his return to *Roches Noires* I thought of 'the fog and damp of the humanist conscience.'

It was already almost dark. We'd just had our tea which was a daily ritual. When my father stopped speaking, grandmother who was over ninety and forgot everything instantly, asked: 'Well, aren't we having tea today?' Her daughter answered her irritably: 'We've just had it. Tea's over!' After a moment's thought, grandmother with the haughty air now inseparable from her bewilderment said as if to herself: 'Nonsense, you idiot! Tea's never over.'